Allan McFadden trained as a secondary school music teacher and has worked as teacher, actor, musician, music director and orchestrator. With fellow Australian, Peter Fleming, he has written several stage musicals: *Airheart, Madame de, Frank Christie, Frank Clarke* and *Noli me Tangere*. His first published novel is *Big Gig in Rock 'n' Roll Heaven*. *Une Autre Fois, Mate!* is the third book in the Dougay Roberre series following on from *Au Revoir, Mate*. All four books are published by Austin Macauley Publishers.

For
Aiste and Milo,
my Czech connection.

Allan McFadden

UNE AUTRE FOIS, MATE!

Some Other Time, Mate!

AUSTIN MACAULEY PUBLISHERS™

LONDON • CAMBRIDGE • NEW YORK • SHARJAH

A CIP catalogue record for this title is available from the British Library.

ISBN 9781398443945 (Paperback)
ISBN 9781398443952 (ePub e-book)

www.austinmacauley.co.uk

First Published 2024
Austin Macauley Publishers Ltd®
1 Canada Square
Canary Wharf
London
E14 5AA

The Dougay Roberre Series

Notes

All characters and situations in *Une Autre Fois, Mate!* are fictional. They bear no resemblance to anyone alive or dead.

The areas and streets of Nice, Cannes and St Laurent-du-var exist, though the buildings occupied by the characters do not.

Marcel Marceau (1923–2007) French mime artist.

Spruik (Australian) means 'to speak in public outside a venue, advertising a performance inside'.

Hotel Abrial in Cannes exists.

Je t'attends (French) means 'I wait for you'.

Merci beaucoup (French) means 'thank you very much'.

Bon soir (French) means 'good evening'.

Ca va? (French) means 'how's it going?'

Maman (French) means 'mother'.

Merde (French) means 'shit'.

Bonne chance (French) means 'good luck'.

Richmond, Collingwood and **Carlton** are suburbs in Melbourne, Australia. They each have football teams which are fierce rivals. The **Sydney Swans** are a football team, transplanted from South Melbourne in the 1980s.

The titles of the three *Mozi-Art 1.0* paintings are Mozart puns. **A Little Night Music** (in German: **Eine Kleine**

Nachtmusik) is a Serenade for Strings; **Rondo a la Turka** is the finale of piano sonata K.331; and one of the characters from his opera, the Magic Flute, is **The Queen of the Night**.

Allez! (French) means 'go!'

If I Were a Rich Man is a song from the musical 'Fiddler on the Roof', music by Jerry Bock and lyrics by Sheldon Harnick.

Scaramouche is a master swordsman, played by Stewart Granger, in the film (1952) of the same name, based on the novel by Rafael Sabatini.

Mate (Australian) is a term for a friend, though it can be used ironically.

Chapter 1

I walked from Gare de Nice, trying not to rush and inadvertently draw attention to myself. I stopped at busy Avenue Thiers, out from the station's entrance, behind people dragging their baggage, hesitant about crossing as passing vehicles drove over the clearly marked white lines, ignoring them.

Come on, come on, my foot was anxiously tapping, because I was now trapped, unable to move forward or back, amongst a growing cluster of tourists.

As well as being surrounded, I felt as if I was caught beneath a dark cloud, which had begun to stalk me the moment I left the station, and was now thickening.

A tourist in front took a deep breath and stepped forward. A car braked. A motorcyclist didn't. He suddenly veered, missing the visitor, the car, and noisily revving away.

I was not intending to bump into anyone, known or unknown, on the way back to the safety of my attic apartment.

I was not planning on stopping to talk with Madame Legrande, the friendly little old lady from downstairs, if she happened to be sitting in a sliver of winter sun, on our oft-shared bench in Place Mozart.

I was not planning on stopping for a convivial chat with M'sieur Pom, at his caretaker's desk in the foyer of my apartment block on Avenue Auber as I walked in.

I was not planning on heading over to *L'Opera Mozart*, the café in which I now owned five percent, and spilling my excitement to Claude Tanguay, my business partner and friend.

And I was certainly not going to call my best mate, Remy Didion, ex-champion boxer, sparring partner and dodgy second-hand furniture dealer, to begin a conversation with, "Hey, Remy, guess what?"

I knew what I *wasn't* going to do. I didn't know what I *was* going to do.

As I crossed over into Avenue Auber, I wrestled the many emotions coursing through me, trying to come to terms with what had just transpired, greatly affected by Audric's generosity. I knew that generosity would resonate for the remainder of my life.

Audric Lefbvre is a man I'd occasionally walked with, and by a series of circumstances, I had managed to solve the forty-year-old disappearance of his baby son and expose the real reason behind his wife's suicide. I was unable to tell him the whole truth, though enough truth to allow him to get himself together and live the remainder of his days in pursuit of a few positive chapters in a tragic life. I understood perfectly his reason for eventually quitting Nice and taking the train to Paris; the one I could now hear behind me leaving the station, heading west to his connection in Marseille.

His final gesture to me was one hell of a way to say goodbye. One moment I was giving him advice on how to possibly live the rest of his days, the next he placed the envelope in my hands, and by the time I lifted my head again, I only saw through a tear of gratitude his disappearing back.

"*A bientot*, mate!" I'd called after him.

Now with each step I looked about, fearing someone would emerge from a darkened doorway or shadow riddled alley to rob me. I automatically clenched and relaxed my fist, the one by my side, several times. Further on, I considered the possibility that it was all a dream.

No, it was no dream. I was heading home to sit alone and contemplate what I was going to do with the papers of authenticity that were inside the envelope I clutched against my chest, next to the small pouch of ten diamonds. *Ten diamonds!* They were the ransom, never delivered to the 'kidnappers' of Audric's baby.

From this moment on, I would no longer have to live hand to mouth. That is, if no one steals them; that is, if no one cons me out of them; and that is, if I don't gamble them away.

Wait a minute! You're not a gambler. You have no desire to enter the casino in Monte Carlo. Get your head together, Dougay! Slow down and stay calm. Breathe, breathe!

Ten diamonds! What would I ever do with them?

You see, Dougay, that's the problem with acquiring sudden wealth. What do you do with it? Spend it or invest it? If so, invest it in what? How are you going to continue to maintain the balance in your life?

I stopped walking and turned back. Perhaps Audric had missed his train and hadn't left the station and I could return the diamonds, informing him, *Thanks Audric, but no thanks. They're only going to bring me a whole heap of worry I don't need.*

Why was I standing still? *How easy a target have you made yourself for a robbery?* Glancing around furtively, I quickly stepped away.

I had no recollection of passing *Villa Fantasia* on my left, my guidepost, which let me know I was one block from home. I looked up and realised I was outside the Belle Epoque building which contained my attic apartment. My irrational fervour eased and I vowed one thing—the diamonds were not going to fundamentally change the man I was. I was still going to remain a jack-of-all-trades, a man for hire. "That's who I am!" I said aloud, reinforcing my belief. "*Dougay Roberre— L'Homme Engager.*"

Thankfully, Madame Legrande was not in Place Mozart across from our apartment block. Thankfully, M'sieur Pom was not at his desk. Thankfully, I did not turn automatically towards *L'Opera Mozart* and Claude.

The elevator was not at ground level so I took the stairs, two at a time, to the sixth floor. Breathing heavily from my rushed ascent, I fumbled my key in the lock. Finally, the door opened and I closed it behind me, leaning my back against it, exhaling such a huge sigh of relief that I'm sure it fluttered the curtains opposite.

I hid the pouch of diamonds under the bottom of the mattress and called Remy to ask if he knew a good locksmith. I felt a security chain and a new dead lock wouldn't go amiss.

His friend, Electro, a wiz at everything electrical and gadgetry, turned up before sunset, and an hour after that, the final bead of worried perspiration evaporated from my brow.

***

I'd never realised how individual the four seasons were until I arrived in France to live permanently. Back home in Sydney, for a little under forty years, I felt there were fundamentally two seasons—winter and summer. Spring and autumn, though present, seemed to be peripheral moments, six to eight weeks at most. Autumn carried summer's lingering aftermath, and spring carried summer's anticipation.

Now, here in Nice, with winter morphing into spring, I could feel my spirits lifting once more. Others could feel the same. Women were beginning to wear brighter colours; children occasionally skipped in the street on the way to school; dog owners lingered in Place Mozart; and shop keepers began rubbing their hands in anticipation of a bumper tourist season.

I'd have loved to be able to say that *L'Opera Mozart* would be benefitting from increased tourist numbers, reportedly some ten million a year; though realistically, my café was no different to hundreds of local cafés throughout the Cote d'Azur. There was no reason for anyone to go out of their way to have their morning coffee with us.

Also, the area where we were located was not in the centre of Nice's tourist district. We were very much a 'locals only' establishment, tucked in between the ocean and the railway station. The café's problem was simply that it needed more 'locals'.

However, I did hold high hopes for the weekend in a fortnight's time. I'd managed to convince Claude to offer a special menu for Friday and Saturday night. Louise Modisette, our newly acquired chef, having risen through our limited ranks from waitress, was preparing a special four-course banquet.

The three of us had been asking all our friends to try to make it. Louise knew no one she was prepared to admit to, though she was coy when asked. Claude had a sister, from whom I'd bought my bed, price waived, when I first arrived here. We had a spiritual connection, so I asked him to invite her, though she had children, and it was difficult for her and her husband to get away at night.

All the other guests had to come from the nefarious collection of misfits I'd stumbled across during my time here. I'd come to Nice to reclaim my French heritage, after being taken to Australia at three years of age by my parents, who had to flee from somewhere in France and enter a witness protection program.

I hoped everyone I knew was going to be hungry in twelve days' time. Not only hungry, I hoped they'd be financially flushed enough to support my, as Claude called it, crazy idea.

I had hosted a successful Christmas day gathering and was hoping those attendees would return and bring with them a friend or two. This dinner would be the first time we'd be hosting paying customers in the newly opened back room. I'd knocked out a bricked-up archway, which linked it to the restaurant, and I'd prepared the walls and painted them. All that was needed now was tables and chairs.

I called Remy, my furniture consultant.

"For a restaurant?" He asked, by way of clarification.

"Yes, for the back room at *L'Opera Mozart*. You remember, you saw it on Christmas Day."

"That was a great day. I really enjoyed it, especially when Angelie arrived."

Angelie Faivre is a woman who'd been a financial high flyer. She had now retired to her farm on top of the mountain beyond Eze. When Remy and I first met her, she'd greeted us standing on her front porch, holding a shotgun.

Remy had some crazy idea that he could have a meaningful relationship with her, by teaching her to box. I had my reservations. Hitting a woman did not seem like the ideal way to cement a permanent caring relationship.

Behind the farmer's clothing, there lurked a thoughtful, intelligent and femininely attractive woman; though Remy faced an insurmountable stumbling block, for Angelie preferred the company of women.

Remy went on, "Particularly, I loved it when all those mad Czech mates of yours turned up with the slivovitz! I'd never sung 'Good King Wenceslas' in the original Czech before."

I wanted to add, *And not with the original melody, either.* I didn't. I didn't need Remy thumping me on the arm the next time we met, telling me, "Everyone's a critic!"

"Remy," I stressed, trying to get him to concentrate on my request, "tables and chairs for the back room?"

"Okay, okay. Some of us like to reminisce about the wonderful life we've lived so far," he admonished falsely. "Not everyone is a capitalist go-getter like you."

"Tables?" I stressed.

"Okay, let me think on it," he muttered and groaned through clenched teeth, making out he was deep in thought. "I'll call you back. I have a friend, and he's heard a rumour about a cousin of his…"

"Okay, call me back." I hung up, not wanting a genealogy lesson of his dubious family tree.

Louise asked with her eyes if we'd be getting furniture. I shrugged, for I had no idea. She wiped her hands on her apron and sat next to me. "Dougay," she began. I sensed a request. I hoped it wasn't about a pay rise. Perhaps Remy was right, I had become a capitalist go-getter.

"What is it, Louise?" I asked, cautiously.

"The weekend we have our banquet, the hostel will have closed by the time…"

"Of course," I said, relieved that she wasn't asking for more money. "I have a proper bed in the second bedroom now. You don't have to sleep on the couch."

"Can I still have the pink duvet?" She laughed. In the short time I'd known her, she'd become part of the 'family'—a member of my small, mainly honest bunch of friends.

My mobile rang. Speaking of 'honest' friends, it was Remy. I was surprised he'd rung back so soon, and even more surprised when he came directly to the point.

"All good, you're in luck," he said, giving me a price.

I took that price to Claude. He began fiddling with the fob pocket of his black waistcoat, saying, "I'll think about it."

"No. I need to know now, Claude. Time is of the essence."

"Now?" He began to fret, rubbing his hand through the non-existent hair he had on top of his head. "What if the tables and chairs don't match the restaurant's existing décor?"

I looked about the restaurant. Louise made a point of opening a blind, letting in light so we could see more clearly. "Décor?" She asked.

"Okay, do it," Claude spluttered. "I don't believe I said that."

"Neither do I!" Louise and I exclaimed simultaneously.

***

Remy's old truck shuddered to a halt.

"You need to fix something down there," I said.

He looked sideways at me from behind the steering wheel. "So now you're a Monaco Grand Prix mechanic?"

It was early evening and light was rapidly fading. Remy had stopped in front of an unlit café in St-Laurent-du-Var, to the west of Nice. He'd deliberately parked the truck in shadow, avoiding the spilled light from the streetlamp.

"Did you bring the money?" He asked.

"Yes, of course."

"Good, give it to me." I lifted my body and took an envelope out from my jeans' pocket. "Stay here," he ordered.

I did as asked, and as soon as the money hit his hand, Remy slid out the driver's door and scooted off around the back of the building. I took my time getting out and leant by the passenger door, waiting; however, not for long. Remy returned carrying two stacked tables, followed by a man carrying a chair in each hand.

"Open the back!" Remy whispered to me. "Quickly, and quietly!"

I did so, and helped him lift in the tables and chairs. I stood there at the rear of the truck looking over the style and colour of the furniture I was buying. They seemed to be okay, possessing no obvious defects. The closer I looked, the more their appeal grew.

They were better than okay. They were actually alright. The chairs had deep red cushions fitted into black metal frames. The tables, with legs made from the same black metal, were glass topped. Remy had delivered above and beyond expectations.

"Come on, more still inside." He grabbed me by the arm and pulled me away. I didn't get inside the restaurant, as everything was stacked in the laneway behind.

Remy and I carried two stacked tables each and the silent man again carried two chairs. After we'd loaded six tables and twenty-four chairs, which thankfully all matched, Remy slid down the truck's roller door, quieter than he had ever done. He waved to the man, who by now was striding away up the street, as if he'd never been near the restaurant.

As the truck began to slowly head home, Remy asked, "Do you think you'd be able to identify that man in a police line-up?"

"No, his face was in shadow all the time."

"Good."

***

Remy parked his truck near the narrow alley behind *L'Opera Mozart* early next morning, before anyone was up and about. Remy's best truck work happens in those peripheral hours before and after bright sunlight. I met him there and we carried the tables and chairs through the fire door, past the stairs, which led to Claude's apartment above, and into the back room.

"I really like the arch," commented Remy. "It's extremely effective." *Effective?* "These tables and chairs will look excellent in here." *What's with all the superlatives?* I thought, figuring there must be a reason for these positive comments.

"Is there any chance of a free coffee?" He asked. I'd figured correctly.

We sat drinking in the back room, at one of my new tables. When the pastry deliveryman knocked on the front door, Remy uttered, "I've work to do; can't be idle like you." He stood. "Saturday afternoon. Be prepared. I've been working on a new deceptive punch." Remy drained his coffee and took off.

Claude came down the stairs and was surprised to see me there, with the pastry delivery under control. He made a point of dramatically looking at his wristwatch. After his poor imitation of Marcel Marceau failed to get a laugh from me, Claude stood back and took in the new tables and chairs.

He circled dramatically, studying them from each of the four corners of the room. He slowly nodded, appreciatively. "Money well spent," he conceded. Repositioning the chair nearest to him by only several centimetres, he muttered, "That's better." He clapped his hands in appreciation of his design skills. "Let's hope the dinner is a success."

Staying on at the café, I helped Louise serve our regular breakfast customers. Well, Louise served and I chatted to them about the weather, French football, soccer and rugby, and the upcoming Tour de France, though to that I mostly listened, as I had no idea about the riders, nor anything else about the cycle race.

A man hovered outside. From across the road, he was looking at the overall structure of the building *L'Opera Mozart* occupied. He studied Claude's apartment above, in relation to the café; and the café in relation to the street and the nearby corner. What also took my eye was the fact that he looked like *un flic*—a cop!

The man was in his fifties, short dark hair turning grey with three-day stubble, bulky body, muscle turning to fat, all wrapped up inside a raincoat. These past few years, I'd say he'd over indulged in stodgy food and red wine. He walked through the café looking about, clearly searching for the toilet. I pointed that it was out beyond the kitchen.

Free loader, I thought as he passed.

He returned after taking what seemed an eternity out there, and sat at one of our outdoor tables. He ordered a coffee. He wasn't a freeloader after all. I can be wrong when it comes to first impressions.

He sipped his coffee, contemplating. After he paid for it, he remained, making mental notes, looking over the buildings opposite. Perhaps my presumption that he was a cop was wrong, for I was now prepared to believe he was a building inspector.

Louise brought the change for old man Hector, a regular customer, who whiled away his mornings here, with or without friends. The change included a ten-euro note and some coins.

I came inside and went to wash the plates and glasses in the sink. A moment later, Hector headed to the toilet. He waved to me as he passed by. I could only manage a smile as my hands were now deep in sudsy water. I was wiping my hands when he returned to his change on the outside table.

"*Mon Dieu!*" Old Hector exclaimed from outside. Turning back to me, he asked, panicked, "Dougay, did you see who took my change? I had a ten euro note here!"

"No, Hector. I'm sorry, I didn't." The only movement I'd seen outside on the footpath was the departure of the cop/building inspector.

"Ahh!" Old Hector spat, angry with himself. He gathered up the remaining coins.

Feeling sympathy for the old fellow, I said by way of compensation, "There'll be a free coffee here in the morning for you."

"You're not to blame," he said, tipping the coins into his pocket. "It's my own fault. Sitting here, sometimes I become too complacent, too comfortable. I think I'm at home."

"Even so," I reassured him, "there'll be a coffee here for you tomorrow morning." I'd let him down. I should have been more aware of what was going on, in and around my café.

"*Merci*, Dougay." He wandered off, again admonishing himself for being blindingly trust worthy. I watched his small grey-headed figure, beret pulled down against the breeze, cross the street and turn a corner, to where I had no idea.

I didn't return to the sink, rather I stood, leaning against an outside table, looking at the buildings opposite and watching the motor bikes, cars and occasional truck going by, thinking of the stranger. I reassessed my appraisal of him. *He wasn't a building inspector, he was a cop. A petty thieving cop! Why do some people in a position of authority break the values inherent in that authority?*

I reminded myself that the line between dodgy cop and petty criminal was a thin one. I'd learned that back in Sydney, and here I'd realised that these two types are universal.

I spread some pate on a broken piece of bread stick, washed it down with fizzy orange juice and called it lunch.

Later, I found M'sieur Pom, a fountain of local knowledge, in his usual spot behind his desk in the foyer of my apartment block, calculator in hand working on the finances of the building.

"What makes a person in a position of authority, run off with someone else's ten euro?" I asked, the act still bugging me.

M'sieur Pom put down his pen. "Because they know they can get away with it," he stated bluntly. He was right, of course. "Is this person a cop or a politician?" He asked, cynically.

"I don't really know. I suspect a cop."

"A corrupt cop has it in his DNA." He scoffed. "Otherwise, he'd have chosen a career path as a legitimate criminal."

I smiled and nodded in appreciation.

"Now, politicians are a very different beast. They carry debt. Not necessarily financial, for they all owe someone, something. How else do you climb that slippery pole? The person holding you up, stopping you from sliding back down once you've got a grip half way, will one day want his *merci beaucoup*."

I nodded, agreeing, for he was spot-on. I wished him *au revoir* and headed to the elevator.

M'sieur Pom continued, "The sad thing about wide spread corruption is that most of it is for small amounts. Why do people sell their souls for such little return?" I couldn't answer that. As I opened the iron gate of the elevator, he called after me, "Why do they blacken their name and reputation by stealing ten euro in plain sight?" I turned back to him, waiting for the well-timed reply to his rhetorical question. He didn't let me down. "Petty corruption is for the petty minded. They should make the deceitfulness worthwhile. Forget ten euro, pocket ten thousand from behind a smoke screen!"

Chapter 2

I woke in the early morning with a cold nose. Vigorously rubbing it, I rolled on to my side, pulling up Princess Grace's pink duvet and snuggling further down into the bed. I couldn't get back to sleep. My ankles could feel the diamonds! I could easily move my ankles off them. However, I couldn't get my mind off them. Even though I had added a new front door lock, I still felt nervous and unsafe with them under my mattress, because I've never, ever, possessed anything of real value. After breakfast, I phoned Remy.

"Are you free this morning?"

"Yes, I'm free, for a price!" He sang. Remy has a special brand of humour.

"Do you feel like a walk?" I asked, not wishing to divulge my true intentions.

"Can we drive instead?"

"I only need to go to the bank. Nearby." So much for concealing my intentions for ringing! "It won't take you long."

Remy thought about it. I could hear him clicking his tongue, as if he had a lot to weigh up. "What's the problem? Is this to do with Electro's new security lock?"

"No. It works well. It keeps everything out, except my worries."

"Mmm," he replied, not really appreciating my concern. "Are you depositing or withdrawing?"

"Do you tell me your personal business?" I asked, wanting to end the verbal logjam. "Like from where you procure your goods of trade, or the history of those tables and chairs?"

"Okay, okay!"

"Meet me in Place Mozart."

An hour later, Remy was there. "It's a long walk from my warehouse to here!" He complained good-naturedly, making a point of rubbing the back of his left leg.

"Sorry for interrupting your day of quality transactions. I could reimburse you to have the soles of your shoes repaired."

"Hunh!" he muttered, stepping off in front of me.

"Why are you leading?" I called after him. "You have no idea where my bank is!"

Remy stopped and waited for me to pass a step-in front. He deliberately placed his right shoulder next to my back and we walked on, as if we were an old-time music hall song and dance duo.

"I'm nervous, that's all," I confessed. "I've never deposited diamonds into a bank before."

Remy sniggered, "Dream on, Dougay, dream on."

Walking there, the fear I had leaving the railway station did not return. With all the friendly banter aside, I was truly thankful for Remy's presence.

At the bank, I hired a safety deposit box and left the jewellery and the accompanying certificates in it. The moment I walked back onto the street, the old care-free Dougay returned. By way of thanks, I bought Remy a coffee at *L'Opera Mozart*. I even tossed in a jam-splattered croissant, for free!

***

With the diamonds safely deposited, all I had to worry about was the first of the two planned dinners this Friday night. Louise had finalised the menu last week, and Claude had created on his computer a printed page, a simple flyer promoting the two evenings, listing the dishes, and the ingredients Louise would be using for each dish.

"One thing is missing, Claude," I said, studying the flyer.

"What's that?" He asked, searching his printed document for a typo.

"There's no Australian wine on the menu."

"What? 'Australian' wine?" He asked, condescendingly.

"Yes—the best in the world!"

Claude was speechless. He 'ummed' and 'ahhed' and then offered some gobbledy-gook about French wine and hundreds of years of tradition and special regions of France, and me being ignorant about the variety of grapes.

"Claude, you failed to mention how the size of the women's feet, stomping the grapes, correlates to the quality of the vintage." Claude ignored my comment. "And, Claude," I paused for effect, "Australian wines are very easy to serve. They come with screw caps!"

"Screw caps! Screw caps!" He was askance. "Philistine!"

I left him floundering in his air of disbelief, and as I smiled with pleasure at having stirred him, I took his printed promos and stuck them in the café's windows. I found myself whistling. Whistling! How long had it been since I'd done that?

Every day, I pointed out the forthcoming event to anyone who dropped in for a coffee or pastry. I even spruiked it to strangers passing by, though I don't believe any of them thought I was serious when I said, "It's a once in a lifetime opportunity."

I'd invited all my acquaintances and friends, though I didn't for one moment expect Francine Delange to attend with her fiancé, the mayor. And I certainly didn't expect Mary-Anne Walton to fly in from New York. I'd have been very happy for Francine to attend and deliriously so if Mary-Anne happened to materialise; however, Nice is a long way to come from Manhattan, even if it is to dine out on a quality beef bourguignon.

Louise took me aside and quietly asked if her special friend could attend. Now I understood why she'd been coy, when we'd first spoken of whom we could invite.

"Of course, it's open for everyone. You do not need my permission, Louise. Does your friend have a name?"

"Martin. We've only recently met. I'll be working in the kitchen, but I'd still like him to come. He doesn't know anyone. Who can he sit with?"

"He can sit with Remy," I said, believing I'd solved her dilemma. "He's friendly to everyone. Does your friend appreciate boxing?"

"No! He's a brainy guy—beautiful, undamaged hands, unlike yours. He's a graduating lawyer, I think."

"If Eloise attends, then he can sit with her." Problem solved. "She's equally friendly."

"Is she beautiful?" Louise asked, concerned.

"Ahh, very much so, I'm afraid." My suggestions weren't easing Louise's concerns at all.

"Perhaps it's foolish of me contemplating. I have to work and he'll be on his own. It's best if he doesn't…"

I clicked my fingers. "He can sit with Madame Legrande. She is a woman for all ages. Does this Casanova have a family name?"

"I don't know. I haven't even kissed him yet!" She hurried back to the kitchen, embarrassed at her openness.

***

On Friday, a little before six, I started pacing. I walked to the front door, back through the café, under the arch, making a loop of the back room, before heading again to the front door.

"Stop that!" Claude hissed. "You're making me more nervous than I already am!"

"You're nervous?" I asked melodramatically. "Whose crazy idea is this?"

On my fifth lap of the café, I stopped in the back room and studied the new furniture. I thought the tables and chairs looked wonderful. Though, what do I know? I then became concerned, hoping they weren't too out of place. "Don't let me down, guys," I said to them.

Louise laughed. "Did you just talk to the tables and chairs?"

"Yes, doesn't everyone?"

She went off to the kitchen, shaking her head. "My boss is a lunatic!" I heard her say to her frying pan.

Madame Legrande was first to arrive. She came through the door beaming, lighting up the room. *My new furniture doesn't stand a chance,* I thought.

"It's only me, Dougay. I'll be bringing people tomorrow evening; however, I had to come tonight. I couldn't let you down on your first night." Even though she was returning tomorrow evening, tonight she'd made a special effort, dressing as if she was off to the opera, though without opera's ostentatiousness.

I handed her a glass of bubbly. "On the house, Madame," I whispered, so Claude was unable to hear. I didn't want him complaining that I was giving away the evening's profits.

"Care to join me?" She asked. "I think you need a drink, dear, you look on edge."

"Is it that obvious?" I asked, taking a flute of bubbly, swallowing it in one gulp.

Oozing sweet chastisement, she said, "Here in France, we tend to sip the bubbly, dear."

"For that moment, I was back in Sydney. I apologise, Madame. I'll imbibe my next glass more in keeping with my sophisticated surrounds."

Madame Legrande laughed and patted my arm. "I do love your false dashes of innocence, Dougay. Will we be having dancing?"

***

My Czech mate, Milovic, stood in the doorway, brandishing a bottle of slivovitz, his country's entry in the world's firewater brewing competition. I'd spent several late evenings at *Vlatava-Elbe*, my favourite Czech watering hole, with his family and friends, trying to put out the heat inside my mouth. I always tried quelling it with dark Czech beer. Occasionally I put out that fire, though never the thump inside my head the next morning. I was grateful Milovic tonight had only brought the one bottle.

Through the door, Milovic was followed by his brother-in-law, Pasha. He also brandished a bottle of the liquid atomic bomb! Milovic's wife, Ulna, and her sister, Ljuba, rushed in from behind them and smothered me in kisses.

"Should I be jealous?" Madame Legrande asked, cheekily. The three women kissed, greeting each other as old friends, having met here at Christmas lunch.

"Madame Legrande," said Milovic, "would you like to taste Czech's most famous export?"

"I thought that was me!" Ljuba exclaimed. We all laughed. I hoped that tonight and tomorrow night there was going to be plenty of it.

"I'm famous as well!" A loud rough voice shouted from the doorway. It was Remy.

With him on either arm, as if escorting them to the opening ceremony of the Cannes Film Festival, was Angelie and Eloise, her friend not his. Remy made a show of having them positioned there. Appreciating the image, my Czech friends applauded. Remy bowed and Madame Legrande went and welcomed them all, kissing them on the cheek.

Who's supposed to be hosting this event? I wondered.

Claude, Remy's old school friend, was as unimpressed with his bravado as I was. "Remy's never changed. He always regarded himself as a lady's man."

"Yes, but do the ladies hold him in the same regard?" I asked. Claude laughed. He was beginning to relax.

I introduced Angelie and Eloise to my Czech mates.

"We met them at Christmas, Dougay!" Milovic explained. "We're all old friends."

Everyone fell into conversation, chattering excitedly, laughing loudly and ignoring me. Made redundant, my spirits lifted when I turned and saw Old Hector and his wife enter. As he introduced me, she over ran his words. "Thank you for inviting us, Dougay."

"You're more than welcome, Madame. All our neighbours are welcome."

"This is what the area needs," said Old Hector. "We need to have some sort of gathering place, a social focus for the community."

That sounded like music to my ears. I'd much rather have a steady stream of loyal locals willing to come here, than try to chase the illusively fickle tourist. "If you enjoy the evening, Hector, spread the word. We're doing it again tomorrow night as well."

A tall dark haired young man stood tentatively by the doorway. Before I could cross to him, Louise, who must have been packing some sort of radar, brushed by me and took him by the arm, turning back to me, fighting shyness and pleasure to announce, "Dougay, this is Martin."

"Do you have a last name, Martin? Only those with a family name are allowed to step over the threshold."

"Ignore him, Martin," Louise admonished. "Dougay thinks he's a comedian."

"Perhaps he is funny in English." Before I could express mock horror, Martin added, "Tetreault."

"I am pleased to meet you, Martin Tetreault. I've heard so much about you."

"No, you haven't!" Louise took me by the arm and whispered, "Don't embarrass me!"

"Never. I'd never do that, Louise."

Louise whispered something to Madame Legrande, then to Martin, quickly poking her tongue out at me, before rushing back to the kitchen.

"So, Martin," began Madame Legrande, her beguiling smile returning to her lips, "I'll have the pleasure of your company this evening. Come on, let me get you a glass of bubbly and let these old folk chat of times past and of failed conquests."

"You're a devil, Madame Legrande," I said, though she made no indication she heard. She eased Martin through the archway and into the back room.

Two friends of Old Hector arrived, accompanied by a couple neither of us knew. "It is so good to see you all," I declared, very pleased that unknown locals were walking through the café's door. Off, behind the bar, Claude was beaming.

In the back room, I caught up with Martin deep in conversation with Madame Legrande. Eye to eye we stood the same height. Beneath neat black hair, he had bright blue eyes and a glowingly warm smile. He said he was filing papers for a law firm, as a casual job, until he finally graduated as a schoolteacher.

I'd never heard of the law firm, then again the only lawyer in Nice I'd heard of, was the one I did occasional jobs for, my sweet Francine Delange.

Everyone settled, happily sitting wherever they pleased, and Claude and I served the first course, after which Louise called from the kitchen, "Dougay, I need help!" Martin followed me in. "Those plates need that sauce, carefully spooned over the meat," ordered Louise. "Careful! It's not as if you're serving up your infamous *Spicey-Ricey*!"

"*Spicey-Ricey* is a bachelor's go-to meal," I explained to Louise, mockingly offended.

"What's in it?" Martin asked, taking the ladle from me and executing the spooning of Louise's sauce to perfection.

"Chopped onions, chopped bacon, tomatoes, mushrooms, all fried in soy sauce with boiled rice stirred in."

"That will never rate a Michelin Hat," he said.

"Maybe not, but it fills a large hole in the stomach. And there's only one plate and one fry pan to wash up afterwards. Besides, I miss Asian cuisine."

"That's not Asian cuisine," admonished Louise. "Now, both of you carry those plates out and tell Claude I need him in here!"

***

Louise, Martin and I spent the hour after everyone departed washing dishes and cutlery in the sink, though Louise's mind wasn't in it. She was too busy studying the young man beside me taking the sudsy plates from my hands and drying them.

"You sit down over there, Louise, you've done enough this evening," I suggested. Without objection she plopped into a chair and exhaled deeply. I turned to Claude, who was wiping down the last of the tables. "Is there any chance of getting a dishwasher?"

"I have one," Claude jauntily replied.

"Where? Upstairs?" I asked.

"No, you!" It's never too late in the evening for my friends to have a laugh at my expense.

"If we buy a dishwasher," Claude went on, "it will have to come out of the profits. Your five percent return will be far lower than anticipated. Besides, we've never needed one." He paused in thought. "Why?" He became suspicious. "What do you have in mind?"

"Nothing; but if these dinners are a success, maybe we could hold them once a month?"

"Let's get through tomorrow night and then see how successful they really are."

Claude possessed the realism of the truly small businessman, whereas I possessed the realism of the truly large dreamer. Together, we have the makings of a truly successful team. I hope!

Outside *L'Opera Mozart*, Louise bid Martin *au revoir*, as I took a long time to turn the key in the lock. I hope they managed a kiss behind my back. Louise waved him *adieu*. She'd still be standing there, watching him disappear into the darkness, if I hadn't have touched her arm and indicated 'home' with my head.

It was well after midnight when we climbed the stairs to the sixth floor, me not wishing to use the old elevator and waking up half the building's occupants. Louise was more than happy to sleep in the second bedroom, as Audric's old bed was preferable to Remy's old sofa in my living room.

"If I wasn't tired before, I certainly am now," commented Louise, taking off her shoes and carrying them into the room.

In my bed, I was nodding off to sleep, when she called out from the other end of the apartment. "Dougay, thank you, for making Martin feel welcome."

"My pleasure, Louise." The earlier tension and excitement of the night was now oozing out of me at a rapid rate. My back was sinking deeply into my bed. I was enjoying the feeling, sleep not too far away.

"He said he had a wonderful evening," she called.

"That's nice, Louise." I no longer had the energy to stay awake. I shut my eyes.

"He said everyone treated him as if he was part of their family."

"That's nice, Louise." I rolled over on my side and pulled the pink duvet up over my head.

Louise said something I didn't quite comprehend, so I didn't reply. She asked a little louder, "Are you asleep?"

"Yes!"

***

Saturday afternoon as usual, I walked up Boulevard Gambetta, under the railway line, to spar with Remy. Sparring had become a regular activity and I looked forward to the faked bouts, for after I stopped swimming in the sea at the end of summer, they were my only form of organised exercise. As Remy let me into his warehouse, he turned from the steel door and I tripped him.

"Hey!" He shouted, regaining balance. "What do you think you're doing?"

"I'm getting in early, before you show me that new punch you're supposed to be developing."

"That's so childish!" He said, thumping me with a straight left to the upper arm.

"Oww!" I exclaimed, rubbing the spot where his blow had landed. Remy might look old, however, he sure packs a young man's wallop.

"That was a familiar, well-developed punch to be going on with."

I continued rubbing.

"A good night, last night," he admitted, without prompting.

"Did Angelie and Eloise enjoy Louise's food?"

"Yes, though not as much as my company."

I snorted.

We danced around each other, throwing punches and dodging the occasional bullet. After the usual thirty minutes or so, I dropped my guard and let him trick me. He threw a jab to my lower back. I knew it was coming, so on impact, I merely laughed.

That was a mistake. Remy pummelled me with a series of fake blows, which only caused me to laugh harder. Soon, we were both spent.

Sitting, breathing quickly and deeply, we were like two over-worked exhaust fans, sweating out the sparring session. We washed off in the large sink in the corner of his warehouse. Drying myself, I asked Remy, "Any furniture arrive this week that I'd be interested in having at my place?"

"No!"

***

Walking away from Remy's warehouse, the Russian *Cathedral Saint-Nicholas a Nice* behind me, I noticed Detective Raphael Legrande, younger son of Madame

Legrande, sitting outside a small cafe. I began to cross the street to say hello.

I changed my mind. He was sitting in conversation with a man, the man who'd stolen Old Hector's ten euro! I kept my head down and took another street to avoid them.

***

That evening, as if on cue, I started pacing the cafe. I needn't have bothered. Louise's cooking, once again, did not let us down. Neither did Martin. Sensing we'd need the same help as last night; he walked in unsummoned and instantaneously became a waiter!

"It was very decent of you, Martin, to volunteer," I told him, genuinely.

"I didn't volunteer. Louise told me I had to come. She said you needed help."

"Did she?" Before I could comment further, Louise was beside me.

"Martin was a great help last night, wasn't he, Dougay? Fifty euro, Dougay, cash, no questions asked. Claude said 'yes'."

"Claude made an immediate decision?" I knew he hadn't. However, once Louise opened wide her eyes and gave me a huge smile, like she was in some old silent movie, I agreed to her subterfuge—anything to bring young lovers together, even if it cost the café fifty euro. To be honest, I was grateful for Martin's help.

Pleasingly, quite a few locals came, total strangers; others I'd seen walking by and never dropping in. Word of mouth was spreading.

Madame Legrande arrived the second time, as promised, sweeping in once again, lighting up the cafe. Tonight, she had her two sons with her. She'd also brought M'sieur and Madame Pom! I was so surprised and grateful that the two women from downstairs came. I hugged them both at the same time, my arms wrapped around them as one.

"Where's my hug, Dougay?" The cunning old fox asked.

As the sly grin on his face grew wider, I replied, "M'sieur Pom, no hug for you. Rather a big sloppy kiss!" I held out my hands to grab both of his cheeks.

"No thanks!" He exclaimed, pulling back from my over-acted gesture. That shut him up.

M'sieur Pom escorted the two ladies into the back room. As she left, Madame Legrande turned back and whispered, "Sip it, Dougay! Sip it!"

Detective Raphael Legrande had with him the beautiful blonde doctor, who had once x-rayed me in hospital, Dr Constance Armand. She possessed that unique quality of being able to walk into a room, turn all heads her way, and without saying a word, make all men realise the combination of her intelligence, beauty and demeanour were on a level none of us could ever attain.

After the few times we'd met, I'd often wondered how Raphael came to be with her. Perhaps there was a side to the detective he never showed me. Then again, being a cop, that arm's length persona was not reserved exclusively for me.

Pierre Legrande, elder brother of Raphael, came with Big Luigi, his bodyguard. Luigi was not here in his usual role of planting himself at the front door and vetting all attendees. Tonight, he was here as a guest, for two much younger women accompanied them.

One of the women was the redhead I'd once seen aboard *The Blue Dahlia*, the yacht of Hollywood producer Harold Kempenski. That one time, she'd been wearing a G-string, below an incorrectly buttoned see-through blouse, so I managed to see quite a lot of her. This other woman possessed equal physical attributes.

Pierre, who ran a collection of high-class call girls under the business name *Milady*, was tonight dipping into his own collection of *fleur de lis* buttock tattooed employees.

Since my time on the Cote d'Azur, I now felt that both Legrande brothers, working either side of the legal fence, had a similar attitude towards me, a friendly begrudging acceptance. The reason? I'd helped save their mother. I'd called for and accompanied her in an ambulance to the hospital after she'd suffered a heart attack next to me on the park bench in Place Mozart.

Another reason was, I'd solved the murder of one of Pierre's girls—an unforgettable blonde, Danielle Hubert.

In the back room, I gathered three tables together and seated the Legrande party around the new formation. They became very noisy, very quickly, and noisier as the wine flowed. Madame Legrande was more than likely the ringleader, because I could hear her shrieks of laughter above the others.

Their bonhomie carried over onto the locals, pulling everyone together, and giving them all, what I'd been hoping against hope, a sense of unified community.

During the evening, while running around, pouring wine, gently ladling sauce over meat, carrying dishes, conversing with everyone, I managed to occasionally stop, stand back and observe their enjoyment. On one of those moments, I found myself alone with Raphael.

"I saw you this afternoon," I said, cautiously.

He picked up on my tone. "Are you now following me?"

"No, I came upon you by chance. May I ask you a question?"

"Of course."

"Who was the man you were having coffee with over in Le Piol?" I waited for an answer.

Raphael took me by the arm and walked me to the far corner of the back room. "May I ask you a question?"

"Of course."

"Why do you ask?"

I thought about that. "We're not going to get very far if we keep posing each other unanswerable questions."

In return, Raphael thought about that. He smiled, enjoying our little game. "The gentleman in question is Detective Bernard St Duprey."

I was right, a cop!

"He was over here in Nice, escorting a prisoner for trial."

"Over here?"

"Yes, he is stationed in Aix-en-Provence. Why do you ask?"

"Is he a friend of yours?" I needed to know this, so I could figure out how I was going to phrase the remainder of our conversation.

"A friend?" Raphael leant into me. "It's very difficult to have a fellow detective as a friend, Dougay. There is far too much trust invested in friendship, as opposed to someone whose job it is to watch your back. So, why do you ask?"

"A couple of days ago, he was paying far too much attention to this building and the buildings surrounding it." Raphael didn't say anything. "He also walked off with another man's change—ten euro."

Raphael snorted. "That makes sense. I don't know him very well. He's there and I'm here. Though we all hear rumours, don't we? My advice to you is to stay away."

"I have no intention of getting any closer than I already have. Dr Armand is looking her usual radiant self. You never speak of her."

"Dougay, mind your own business." The cop in Raphael had resurfaced. He turned to go, our *tête-a-tête* over.

"What if I were to ask her to dance?" I asked, cheekily.

He stopped. "There's no music."

"I could sing."

He looked at me with a knowing twinkle in his eye. "Apart from her degree in medicine, she has a secondary degree in music. I'm sure your singing would not impress her. You'd only drive her back to my arms. Besides, you don't look like a dancer to me."

"I must be a lover, then."

Raphael laughed, patted me on the shoulder and shook his head in disbelief at the nonsense we'd both been speaking. He returned to his table and I returned to the kitchen.

Later, his brother, Pierre, took me to one side. "I haven't heard the detective laugh like that since he put a frog down my back when we were kids." I couldn't believe anyone had ever done that to Pierre Legrande and lived to see another sunrise, even at a young age. "What were you talking about?"

"Another cop who's in town delivering a prisoner," I said, as vaguely as possible.

"Bernard St Duprey?"

"You know him, then?" I asked, surprised. I shouldn't have been surprised. Between them, these brothers knew everything that was going on in Nice!

"He is a corruptible cop, with a petty criminal for a brother, and an even pettier one for a first cousin. And, believe it or not, by day they are uniformed officers of the law. Avoid them, Dougay. If you don't, you'll be scraping shit off your shoes for weeks."

I nodded at his helpful advice. "It's nice to see your redhead once more. What's her name again?"

"Nice try, Dougay, nice try." He left me for her. I was destined never to know the name of this striking woman.

Madame Legrande found me. She kissed me on the cheek, saying that it was past her bedtime and next time we were to do this dinner evening, we should think of dancing. Madame Legrande clearly misses the old days.

"Dancing? I was only talking to Raphael about that!"

She left with the Poms, saying, "Perhaps I'll see you in the morning in Place Mozart?"

"I'll be there, Madame."

Once again, well after midnight, Martin walked off into the darkness, and Louise came back to sleep the night at my place. We walked there very pleased with ourselves.

"I'm very impressed with what you've done this weekend, Louise. Claude and I could never have managed such an enjoyable feast without you. You are a superb chef in the making."

Louise hugged my arm delightedly, in a daughterly kind of way.

Back home in bed, I was just nodding off when she asked, "Dougay, any chance you'd rent me this room?"

Chapter 3

On Sunday morning, Louise returned to her hostel, and early Monday, she knocked on my apartment door with a loaded duffle bag. I hoped she hadn't stolen it from some unsuspecting tourist. Standing there, she heartbreakingly smiled like a waif, who'd stumbled across my door by chance and needed taking in. Her eyes were full of hopeful promise. The only thing missing was the falling snow accompanied by the sound of a distant plaintive violin.

"I don't remember saying 'yes'," I said, putting up a false wall of resistance.

"You didn't say 'no'." She had a point. "I promise not to compromise your love life."

I laughed. "You cannot compromise something which doesn't exist!" I stepped from the doorway and letting her in, took hold of her duffle bag and carried it to her bedroom. "You'll have to share the bathroom until I get the one down this end cleaned up."

Once I dropped her duffle bag on the floor, she unpacked and set about cleaning the second bathroom! I helped by removing the two empty suitcases I'd brought with me from Australia. I slid one under my bed and heaved the other on top of the old wooden wardrobe Remy had sold me when I first took up residence.

There was nothing inoperable in the second bathroom—water flowed out of taps and ran downhill, which is always preferable. On its path, it didn't clog or back up. The showerhead was a reasonable size and the water pressure was the equal of mine.

Louise burrowed in under the kitchen sink, finding a bottle of cleaning fluid, and set about scrubbing all the old wall tiles in the bathroom, which were of a design and quality that didn't need replacing. After three hours, they sparkled.

"I'll look around for a new shower curtain. That one's torn." What I meant was, I'll ask Remy if he had one amongst the stuff in his warehouse. In my wardrobe, I found two near-matching bath towels which I gave her. Louise was still short of a duvet and bed sheets.

By mid-afternoon, she'd prepared her bedroom and bathroom. I took her downstairs to introduce her to M'sieur Pom. He took me aside and said, "I like her. She's not battered and bruised, unlike the other women you bring back here." Before I could say anything, he added, "And she's a wonderful chef!"

Madame Legrande's door opened. "Ah, Louise, welcome to Avenue Auber." She gave Louise a hug and a kiss.

"Madame Legrande, how did you know that Louise was moving in?" I stopped and gave her a knowing look. "Did you put the idea into her head?"

"Dougay, I worry about you all alone up there in the attic."

I playfully wagged my finger at her and Louise giggled. Upstairs, I gave Louise my second set of keys and explained how my new deadlock worked.

"How much do you want me to pay?" she asked.

"It's okay. Just clean the floors; do my laundry; iron my shirts; cook my breakfast; wash the dishes." She looked at me askance. "Just joking; nothing."

"Nothing?" She did not believe me.

"Louise, I do not want your money, five percent of which, I'm paying you."

"Are you sure?" She asked, giving me a chance to change my mind, though hoping I wouldn't.

"Yes, I'm very sure. I'll be thankful for the company. I need your endless conversational stream to send me off to sleep each night."

"You are too kind-hearted, Dougay."

"Yes, and as all my friends tell me, one day it will bring me undone."

***

Accompanied by Louise, I walked over to Remy's warehouse in search of a shower curtain, a duvet and sheets. I banged on the roller door. He pushed open the steel one.

"A what?" Remy exclaimed. "A shower curtain? I'm not a bathroom emporium!"

Disheartened, Louise turned from the door. Remy watched her walk several steps.

"Stop!" He shouted. Louise turned back. "Come on," he said, "you're just in luck, Louise. A shipment of shower curtains was only passing by yesterday. The truck flipped and by a miracle, twenty or thirty of them landed inside this warehouse."

Louise looked sceptically at us and asked, "Which one of you taught the other?"

We both laughed and Remy led Louise into his Aladdin's cave. He wove his way between all the stuff back there, and without the aid of compass or map, put his hands on a new duvet and sheets! Louise and I followed him across to the other side of the warehouse, where there were several brand new plastic shower curtains decorated in various bright and gaudy patterns.

He spread them out a little so Louise could select one.

She found a red floral one she liked. "Will this one look okay?" She asked me.

I draped it over Remy's shoulder and wrapped him up in it. "Remy looks lovely behind it," I said. "So, you'll look sensational! We'll take this one, Remy."

Remy unwrapped himself and folded it up, tying a string around it. I paid him. Pocketing the euro, he said, "Next time, Dougay, text me before you're dropping over and I'll try to find a laugh for you."

I laughed mockingly. "Oh, one other thing, Remy, Louise will need a wardrobe and a chest of drawers. Free delivery, of course."

***

During those days following our successful dinners, the smell of spring seemed to be everywhere. I was sitting in Place Mozart with Madame Legrande and she commented on it. "Farewell, February," she said. "I've always loved the first taste of spring. Don't you feel the same when you farewell February?"

"No, Madame," I said, quietly. I hoped I hadn't sounded as if I was disagreeing with her, so I explained, "In Sydney, February means very hot days with several huge downpours of evening rain. I never wanted those hot days to disappear."

"Ah. It must be odd living underneath the world, where everything is the wrong way around."

"Madame, have you ever thought that perhaps you, up here, have it the wrong way around?"

She squeezed my arm. "Touché!"

***

On Thursday evening, I was sitting in *L'Opera Mozart* with the lights out, contemplating. I was revisiting an idea I'd had a few weeks ago, and was trying to imagine it, in play, inside the café. I was deliberately sitting in the dark, as lights overhead do not let my imagination take flight. Louise had left an hour before and Claude had gone off to his sister's place to spend the night babysitting her children.

From beyond the kitchen, down the corridor, there was a flash. It took my eye and as I climbed from my chair, I saw another sliver of torchlight on the corridor ceiling. I rose and quietly stepped beneath the arch across the back room.

Through the window above the exit door, the beam was being thrown from side to side. Then it turned off. I tiptoed to the fire exit and savagely tossed my weight against the bar. The opening door fell away, and I stumbled into the narrow alley behind.

A man swung around, turning on the torch into my face. I instinctively shielded my eyes behind my raised hand.

"What are you doing?" I asked, as unthreateningly as possible, making out I was half-asleep.

He indicated that I should stay where I was and reached inside his jacket. I hoped he wasn't about to pull out a gun. He didn't. He pulled out a police identification and raised it for me to see.

"I'm checking on the security of this building. It all seems perfectly in order," he said in an unwavering, unflustered authoritative voice. "Nothing to concern you."

"Who are you?" I asked, though I knew perfectly well who he was.

"Police officer; didn't you recognise the I.D.?"

"Name?"

"I won't keep you. Enjoy your evening." He turned off the torch and walked out of the alley.

I waited until Detective Bernard St Duprey was out of sight. I then looked overhead and around. *What had he been searching for?* Even though I'd often been out here carrying rubbish to the large bins down the end, I'd never really taken in the detail of the buildings enclosing the laneway.

Above the cafe's rear exit door, there was the window I'd seen the torchlight flashing through. The only other window was situated on the floor above, Claude's apartment. The buildings on the other side of the alley had no windows.

In the dim moonlight, the guttering on the rooftops appeared to be intact. I looked down at my feet. All the old paving stones, though uneven, were in place. Everything was as the cop had said, secure.

I returned inside firmly closing the exit door. Back in my chair, I wondered what a detective based in Aix-en-Provence was doing snooping around buildings in Nice.

***

On Friday, I was stacking dishes away for the evening, when Raphael Legrande phoned me. "I was impressed with you the other night."

"Thank you," I automatically answered. *Why would he phone me to tell me this?*

"You were moving among your guests, taking an interest, keeping everyone happy, like a professional."

"Where is this leading, Raphael?"

He cleared his throat. "Once a year, a society art lover, Madame Antoinette St Romain, holds a charity art auction at *Le Grande Nice*. Her society reserves the entire restaurant for the evening. My Maître d', Maurice Pontbriand, whom you've met, always attends as a guest. I was wondering if you'd like a job for the evening—greeting people at the door, and checking off their names against the invitation list. I'll pay you."

"Pay me?" I didn't hesitate to say, "Yes." I also didn't tell him I can't read French, though I reasoned that wouldn't be a problem, as it was only a guest list I'd be perusing and not the first hand written draft of *Les Misérables*.

"Be at *Le Grande Nice* on Sunday, around five. I'll show you the layout of everything." Before he hung up, I asked him if he also needed a waitress for the night.

"Louise?"

"Yes."

"Both of you wear black."

***

Saturday, mid-morning, leaning on an outdoor table at *L'Opera Mozart,* I was staring vacantly, preoccupied with my thoughts of Detective St Duprey standing opposite, studying the buildings that first time I'd become aware of him. *What was he doing over there? How long had he been there before I noticed him? Why?*

A shouted, "Hey!" interrupted my train of thought.

I turned quickly, dropping my cleaning cloth onto a table. An angry man, a complete stranger, was nearly upon me. Several paces behind him trailed a woman.

"Monsieur?" I took a cautionary step back. "How may I help you?"

"You!" He spat. "I want to talk to you."

He changed his mind about conversing, instead throwing a telegraphed right-handed punch!

I stepped aside and let his momentum carry him forward onto the café's outdoor table, which broke his fall. He'd been drinking, and not just the one. I let him find his own way up onto his feet, though that was not going to happen immediately.

The woman behind, called out, "Ronaldo!" Her voice also sounded as if it had been well lubricated this morning.

Ronaldo, splayed across the table, spewed forth up at me, "Stop screwing my wife!"

I looked at the woman, indicating that clearly her husband was mistaken.

"He's not!" She shouted at him. "I don't know this waiter!"

"Don't lie to me!" He stood ungainly. When he'd found some sort of balance, he spat back at her, "You are. You are!"

"He's not! He's not!" The woman shook him, trying to drive some sense into him. "It's the café further down the street. That's where I'm screwing the waiter!"

Chapter 4

Le Grande Nice is an up-market restaurant co-owned by the Legrande Brothers, which they inherited from their father. From what I'd been told, he'd had his fingers in many pies, not all baked on the right side of the law. It was the only enterprise that Raphael, detective, and Pierre, entrepreneur, were partners in. That's what Raphael told me the night he took me to dinner there and planted in my head the germ, which eventually led to me depositing the ten diamonds into a safety deposit box.

When wishing to ask me to do something for them, they both initially began on a tangent, skirting the point, testing me out until they felt comfortable with what they were proposing. Madame Legrande had assured me that it was a trait inherited from their father, not her, and that I was not to take it personally.

I could tell this evening's job offer was legitimate, not part of a tangent, the moment I walked in the door with Louise and was handed the extensive guest list. I glanced through it. The mayor's name was there and so was Francine's. My heart skipped.

There was a banner behind the lectern I was to stand at, immediately inside the door. Because of my limited French literacy—I only speak French, courtesy of my parents—I asked Louise to read the banner for me.

"The Society for the Advancement of Artistic Expression, Endeavour and Realisation on the Cote d'Azur." The Society's name did not slip fleetingly from her tongue. *"President: Antoinette St Romain. Proudly sponsored by The Nicois-Massena Group."*

Raphael greeted Louise and me. "Congratulations, Louise. It was a superb meal the other night. You're a wonderful chef." Gallantly, Raphael kissed her hand. Where had the police detective, with the big boots designed for kicking heads, gone to?

"Be careful, Dougay, I might poach her from you." He took her arm to lead her towards the kitchen's serving area.

Leaving, she managed to whisper, "Classy!"

I managed to whisper back, "Loyalty!"

I was early, as requested by Raphael, so I stood at the lectern and studied the guest list. It was a who's who of Nice. If a bomb went off in here tonight, there'd be no one left to run the city; or the criminal activities within it; or to report on the explosion, for at that moment a reporter and accompanying photographer walked in as if they were invited. I tried to hold them up. Raphael saw, came over and said it was okay for them to slide in.

Passing by me, the reporter uttered, "I'm Mimi Benoit!" The name meant nothing to me. She was one of those old-fashioned newspaperwomen, who in the past would have reported on 'family issues'. I assumed she'd now been lumbered with 'social events' and the 'arts'. She may have been 'old fashioned'; however, she was not old and her smile to Raphael, which lit up her face, wiped years from my first impression of her.

Some people think they are equally at home in high society events and low-life dives. Big Luigi entered. "You got an invitation?" I asked, cheekily. "Tonight is a classy event. Do you think you can just swan in here, because your boss owns half the place?"

Looking about the room, checking that it was safe to bring in Pierre, he murmured to me, "What are you doing here? Is this the last stop before the morgue?"

Luigi and I have history. You could say we have a mutual respect for each other, though at times I didn't think he was aware of that. On our first meeting, he tried to manhandle me. However, before he could get his large mitts on my throat, I hit him with a straight left to the chin. He hit the floor, out cold. Up to that point, he didn't know he had a glass jaw.

He turned from me and opened the door. Pierre Legrande entered, nodded to me in recognition, and didn't wait to have his name checked. On his right arm was the gorgeous nameless redhead, and on the other, the equally gorgeous blonde from Louise's Saturday night dinner. I gathered Pierre had permanently replaced Danielle Hubert in his collection.

As he entered the restaurant proper, Luigi took the blonde by the arm. *To lighten Pierre's load*, I laughed to myself. As they walked from me, I childishly admired the blonde woman's bare back and Pierre's eye for distinctive looking employees.

Punctually at six, the first invited couple pushed open the door. If they were all going to look like this pair, it was going to be a night full of the 'beautiful people' of Nice. He had a rugged square jaw, with dark close-cropped stubble. His dinner suit fitted the developed chest and biceps like a glove. I'm sure his partner also spent every morning in the gym, developing every asset she possessed, for tonight they were on display. She wore a tight-fitting black dress with a plunging neckline. Thank God, it stopped plunging where it did, for the fire brigade would have to have been called to extinguish the spot fires emanating from beneath many a bow-tied collar. I ticked off their names on my list with the shakiest tick I'd ever committed to paper.

I saw reporter, Mimi Benoit, interview them, writing down a quote on her notepad. Then the photographer clicked the couple, arms around each other; their brilliantly sparkling sets of teeth shining like two follow spots at the opening night of the Cannes Film Festival.

Raphael came purposefully to me, accompanied by a statuesque woman, late fifties, dark hair with a streak of grey. The streak couldn't be natural, as it was too precisely defined. She had an imperious look about her, knowing she unquestionably belonged everywhere she set foot. In short, she was confident, stately, and reeking of understated wealth. If only someday I could grow to develop those qualities.

"Dougay, this is Madame St Romain," Raphael said. "Madame, this is your Maître d' for this evening, Dougay Roberre."

"So pleased to meet you," she gushed. "But please, let's not be formal, call me Antoinette, everyone does." She shook my hand. She had a grip. She looked past me onto the darkened street, as if expecting someone.

No one appeared, so her gaze turned back to us. She smiled disappointedly and returned inside.

"Antoinette is the president of the Society," explained Raphael. "She is extremely well known here on the Riviera—a collector, connoisseur, and patron of the arts."

"I've heard her family name, somewhere."

"She's the sister of the mayor," explained Raphael, as if I should have known.

I clicked my fingers in realisation. "Of course." I knew tonight was going to be an eye opener for me. I hoped I'd begin at last to understand part of the spider's web of Nice's society.

"Does she always dress as a man?" I asked.

"She is also well known in another sort of circle. She is a great promoter of all artistic endeavours, female. I'm told her private parties are renowned among certain people of a certain persuasion on the Cote d'Azur." He winked, though he needn't have bothered, as I understood perfectly what he had implied. Then again, detectives do like to beat you over the head, and rarely with subtlety.

Guests arrived whom I'd never heard of. However, their names were on the list, so I ticked them off. Judging by the consistent high standard of dress, tonight was a serious event on the social calendar of Nice's elite. There was also a lot of sparkling stuff hanging off ears, wrapping around wrists, and dangling from necks.

I glanced up and Francine was before me. I smiled spontaneously, delighted to see her once more. Rather than ignore me, she smiled back, genuinely surprised that I was here.

"Oh, darling," she said, turning around the man with her. "This is Dougay. He does some work for me. Dougay, I'm surprised to see you here."

"Ah, Madame Delange, lately your job offers have dried up. I have to pick up what I can."

"Well, I'll have to do something about that, then," she said, matter of factly. "I can't have you picking up any odd bits and pieces." Was she referring to work or other women?

"Dougay, be warned, odd bits and pieces can prove damaging to your health." Yes, she was referring to other women. "This is my fiancé, Maurice St Romain."

"Ahh, Monsieur, I met your sister a little earlier."

His Honour the Mayor did not reply. His Honour the Mayor did not take my offered hand. His Honour the Mayor walked off, leaving Francine by the lectern with me.

"I apologise for him," she whispered. "He is often short with people." She leant into me and dropped her voice further. "I have arrived—though not yet permanently—one step at a time. I hope to marry the egoist in the summer."

And then she was gone, leaving behind her unintended small dagger. As I watched her walk away, I withdrew it from my heart.

To be honest, I'll never be over Francine. The prospect of Mary-Anne returning in the summer, always seemed to take a back seat whenever Francine crossed my mind. Though the two times I'd been with Mary-Anne, Francine never entered my thoughts. I guess I am fundamentally a one-woman man. I can only think of one of them at a time. Apart from when I pose myself the question: *Which woman do I care for more?* Then they both vie equally for my undivided attention, and subsequently drive me to despair.

A man rushed in, breathlessly asking, "Has the mayor arrived?" I pointed further into the restaurant. He moved off.

"Sir!" I called after him. He turned. "Do you have an invitation?"

"I don't need to show you an invitation! Don't you know who I am?" Without waiting, he answered his question. "I am the mayor's personal secretary!" He eased his short stature upwards.

"I'm Guy Germaine." I checked the guest list. He was on it, though next to his name there was no note which read: 'Dickhead'.

Guy Germaine was very gay. Francine had told me that her fiancé had a gay lover. I wondered if this was him. He struck me as being extremely volatile. If I was one for making politically incorrect comments, I'd have nicknamed him: 'Gay Guy'!

The numbers were swelling, the champagne was being passed around by Louise and others dressed in servant black, and the vocal level in the restaurant was rising. The evening was well underway. I noted that rich people seemed to enjoy themselves exactly as poor people do—laughing, drinking, and carrying on. The extra price on their ticket doesn't automatically guarantee a higher level of fun, compared to what can be achieved by us gutter dwellers.

Eloise Pittard entered on the arm of a man I recognised. He was the recipient of six hundred- and fifty-thousand-euro Francine and I had brought back from Milan. It had been a weekend of subterfuge, with the Saturday evening dinner being highlighted for me, by a fistfight in the street outside our hotel, courtesy of the duplicity of the dodgy Italian businessmen, the Mascati twins. This new arrival didn't remember me.

Eloise gave me a reserved smile, slightly nodding her head. She was one of Pierre's girls and she was working this evening. I was working as well. We both knew our place.

"Do you have an invitation, I may see please, Sir?" I asked in my best detached and uninterested voice.

I checked his name. Slightly shorter and older than me, he went by the name of Paul Villan.

"Enjoy the evening, Sir, Mam'selle."

Paul Villan put his arm on Eloise's back and guided her forward into the crowded restaurant, though I got the impression Eloise knew exactly where she was going, as she'd no doubt been here before and many other high-class places like it.

I turned, surprised. "Doctor Armand, welcome. A pleasure to see you once more. Are you well?"

"Very well, Dougay. What a wonderful evening last week. The food was superb and I was genuinely surprised by the old-fashioned nature of it all. It's been a while since I've enjoyed the simplicity of that."

"Thank you, but a lot of the credit goes to Louise."

"Yes, of course. Us doctors often forget the importance of the nurses involved in the operation. Is Raphael inside?"

I said he was, and gestured into the restaurant. She went off to find him.

I turned back to the front door. "Madame Legrande! I didn't know you'd be here this evening, but then again, whose restaurant, is it?"

"Dougay," she began, her smile lighting up her face, "I'd like you to meet Monsieur Albert Tarrant." I greeted the distinguished grey-haired gentleman with a courteous nod.

"Dougay is a dear, dear friend, Albert. He once saved my life."

Monsieur Tarrant nodded sagely or distantly; I couldn't tell. Perhaps he was slightly deaf, or distracted by the people gathered inside. As they walked away, she let go of his arm and returned to me. He continued on, to speak with Madame St Romain.

"No need to worry, Dougay," Madame Legrande said, reading my mind. "He thinks he's Yves Montand, but you and I both know he's not." She gave me a wicked wink and disappeared into the crowd to join her partner for the evening.

A gentleman wearing glasses a size too big, giving him a slightly comical edge, entered with a woman. They did not hold hands, and her arm wasn't entwined through his. I wasn't interested in his name, though he was on the guest list. I was far too interested in the beauty of the woman.

She was my height, and she was Eurasian. She had the black hair colouring and clear skin of a fine porcelain Chinese doll and the height and stature of a Parisian showgirl. What a combination! I committed her name to memory, *Sue-Lin Cambridge*. In a room full of beautiful women, it is very difficult to stand out from the pack. Sue-Lin did.

Beau Andrews! What was he doing back in Nice? I had come across him on *The Blue Dahlia*, where he had verbally belittled me. I knew far more about him than he did of me. I knew he loved to get beaten by, or give a beating to, gay buffed men. I also knew of his chauffeuring role in the assault on Eloise Pittard and the murder of Danielle Hubert. I said nothing, my face blank face, pretending he was a stranger. He was dressed as if he was a 1930s' gangster from a black and white movie, though Beau Andrews was no Jimmy Cagney.

Beau was accompanied by another man, with short cropped, greased back hair, baggy cream trousers, and a grey vest over a matching cream shirt. Round bookish glasses covered the face. On closer look, I inhaled rapidly, quickly looking about, hoping the intake wasn't noticeable.

The names on the guest list read: 'Nick and Nora Charles', however I recognised this 'man' as the film actress, Belinda Swann!

Antoinette St Romain saw the couple and was quickly over to them. Perhaps they were the ones she'd been earlier scanning the footpath for. She shook hands with Beau, though to Belinda she gave a kiss. There was nothing special in that. It's just that the kiss lingered for a long time and their arms went around each other lovingly. They'd met before and quite possibly *sans clothing*.

It was an evening for the high class and the low class to rub shoulders. No one arrived who was more low class than Felicity Deschamps, the ex-wife of the disgraced ex-deputy mayor. I'd met her when she'd posed as Madame Ardoin, feeding me Pierre Legrande's bullshit about the missing Eloise being her lost niece. She'd forgotten who I was, and probably that she'd ever performed the masquerade. At times, I'm thankful for not having such a memorable visage.

"This gentleman is not on the list," she explained. "Next to my name it should read: 'and guest'. This man is the well-known painter, Lautrelle Martin."

"Madame Felicity," began the artist, "of course I'm on the list." He paused, looking at me. "I am one of the featured artists. My work is being auctioned tonight."

Before Felicity could apologise for her oversight, a raspy female voice called from behind them, "Lautrelle!" The voice belonged to a woman in her late forties, with wild uncombed hair, or rather carefully teased hair, giving her a strikingly primitive persona. "Still painting realistic shit?" She asked.

"You're stoned, and drunk, Gabrielle," said the well-known painter, though I didn't know him.

"Correct with one thing, darling. Where's the bubbly?"

"Madame?" I called after the obnoxious woman. She turned back looking at me for the first time. She crooked her finger and beckoned I come to her. I did. I bent forward to hear her whisper.

She didn't whisper. She grabbed me suddenly on the nuts! I sprang back. She laughed, uproarishly. I turned away from her. She then pinched me on the ass!

"Gabi! You're disgusting!" Lautrelle reprimanded.

"Get fucked, darling!"

"Such language!" Felicity remonstrated.

"Knowing you, Felicity, you're already planning to. But, tonight you'll be missing out." She headed inside, after calling back, "You'll need to find another man; Lautrelle's gay!"

The painter looked at me. "Monsieur, I apologise for her. Gabrielle Surmount is a legend on the Cote d'Azur. Not always for her paintings!"

Gabrielle Surmount had the ability to turn heads when entering a room. She did it with a noisily over-bearing exuberance—the opposite approach to the refined grace of Dr Armand or Francine Delange or Sue-Lin Cambridge. Gabrielle Surmount had been to these types of events before, because the first person she greeted was the drinks waiter.

Armed with two glasses of bubbly, she surged forward into the crowd. Men pulled back as she approached. Moses could have utilised her skill to advantage when he was parting the Red Sea.

Felicity and Lautrelle entered the restaurant's main room as a group of others arrived. I crossed all their names from the list in one grand gesture, smiling and indicating Louise waiting for them with her tray of bubbly flutes.

After some time, the arrivals thinned and then stopped, so I went and stood to oversee the people inside, mingling, drinking, engaged in conversation. It is very interesting to stand detached, totally sober, observing snatches of behaviour.

I saw the sense of unease in the body language of Francine, as she stood with her fiancé and listened to him converse with other similarly conservatively suited men. The mayor was paying particular attention to Albert Tarrant. They seemed to go back a long way, because they were extremely comfortable in each other's company, speaking across Francine, not bothering to include her in the conversation.

Francine's eye caught mine, and with a small tilt of her head, she expressed the boredom she was tolerating.

Now and then, over several minutes, I caught sight of Antoinette St Romain move around the room, gathering up the artists present, and corralling them towards the small raised platform, from where the speeches and auction would take place.

I saw Eloise become startled.

I saw Dr Armand, completely relaxed and laughing on the arm of Raphael. I had no idea if either had been married before, or this relationship was new, formed later in life. No matter what their past, they appeared as the perfectly happy couple.

I saw Beau Andrews in earnest conversation with the mayor's personal assistant, Guy Germaine. I saw him cut the secretary from the pack and move him off into a corner.

I saw Eloise move away, as far as possible, from the incognito Belinda Swann.

I saw Luigi looking about, more concerned with who might be in the room posing a threat to Pierre, rather than what the blonde on his arm might be saying.

I saw Belinda Swann, standing with Madame St Romain, be lovingly welcomed by two ladies who'd approached her. One of the ladies in that exclusive circle could not keep her eyes from the Hollywood star. *Belinda's won a heart for the night,* I deduced.

I lingered my gaze on Sue-Lin Cambridge, as she stood, conversations drifting around her, seemingly uninterested, her head above most of those gathered there. I wondered why she and Francine, two of the most beautiful women in the room, were treated distantly by the men gathered around them.

I saw Eloise in a far corner ending a phone call. She hurriedly put away her mobile and glanced about to see if anyone was noticing. She did not see me seeing her from across the crowded room.

And then it hit me. I finally had formulated the idea for *L'Opera Mozart* that had been eating away at me these past few weeks. I would have my own 'art event'. It would be a collection of paintings of the famous composer. Though not merely that, for the paintings had to be of a humorous, even satiric nature. In that moment, I decided to name the event: *Mozi-Art.*

Chapter 5

"Madame, would that be over there, incognito, that American film actress?" I quietly asked Antoinette St Romain, knowing full well it was. I was curious as to how this matron of Nice Society knew the young American star.

"Shh," she whispered. "Yes, she's a naughty poppet, that one." I made no comment, hoping that Madame St Romain would continue. She didn't disappoint.

"She flew in last week, bless her soul, to celebrate my sixtieth birthday. The dilettante in me precludes me from telling you what she gave me, though it was wicked, wicked, wicked of her.

"Sixty? Why, Madame, you do not look a day over twenty-one." I can turn on the charm when I wish to.

She laughed. "Is that flattery, Monsieur?" I smiled and gave her a wink. "I'm sure you're a gentleman of the world, Monsieur, and therefore I say to you, as such, that young scamp and I go back a long way. I love her, or rather, I loved her.

"She was far too experimental for my liking. Once in a while, on a special occasion, I can enjoy it, like last week, though she's far too relentlessly demanding. To be honest, she frightens me with some of her sexual desires. Fortunately for her, she doesn't frighten a few of my friends and acquaintances.

"I like to think she comes to Nice to visit me. Oh, don't get me wrong, she did. Though she also comes to taste the delicacies other French women offer."

I now had a strong sense that Antoinette St Romain, after a glass or two of bubbly, loved to talk. I was in a mood to let her.

"It's a diverse planet we live on, isn't it, Monsieur? American stars, of all sexual persuasions, can hide out here in Europe, away from their childish and scandal mongering media. They can let their hair down, and in a sense become someone else, or find their real self, away from the spotlight.

"It's only around film festival time that that rapacious American lot, with their intrusive pens, cameras and microphones set foot in the place. I shudder annually, when that time comes around."

I appreciated everything Madame St Romain was saying, though I thought 'poppet' and 'scamp' were rather naïve terms to describe the cruel and perverted ways of Belinda Swann.

Raphael brought me a glass of champagne, which was kind of him. As I took it, I had second thoughts. "I'm on duty, aren't I?"

"Everyone who's attending will be here by now. And what riff-raff is going to gate crash a society art event?" He turned from me. "Madame St Romain, your committee members have been asking if you're ready to commence the proceedings."

"Oh yes, of course. One forgets that this evening is not only concerned with champagne, canapés and scintillating gossip. There's a serious side to our frivolity, as well."

Raphael and I watched her return to the crowded restaurant. He asked, "Can you do a favour for my brother?"

I looked at him, wide eyed. "I thought you never speak with your brother."

"I speak to him, when on these premises," the detective admitted, "as he's co-owner, remember?"

I nodded wryly. "What's the favour?"

"Have you noticed that exotic-looking Asian woman?"

"Eurasian," I corrected. "No, I haven't seen her."

He laughed. "Okay, yes—the tall model, Eurasian."

"The one with long legs."

"Okay, okay! She needs escorting home, back to her hotel, after the evening is over."

I looked at him, puzzled. "If I remember correctly, she came with someone, a man wearing overly large glasses."

"He made an instant impression on you?"

"No, she did."

Raphael ignored my carry on. "The man she accompanied is the manager of the franchise: 'Water Babies'. Later in the evening, he will be in a long conversation with my brother, and therefore unable to escort her back to her hotel. Have you heard of 'Water Babies'?"

"No."

"It's a swimwear boutique. There are three on the Cote d'Azur. The model is in town promoting a new label, as she's their international face. The man she came with has taken on her product to sell in the stores. Can I say you'll do the gentlemanly thing?"

"How long is their meeting going to be?"

"As long as it takes. Look at the man she came with. Do you think he has enough money behind him to own boutiques on the seaside promenades of Nice, Cannes and Monaco?"

"Pierre really owns the stores? And he's Pierre's employee?"

"Dougay, you're a slow learner, though you do eventually get there. Yes, my brother is having a catch-up meeting with him, when tonight's function is concluded."

"Of course I'll walk her home. If you give me fifty euro, I'll take her home in a taxi."

"Not necessary. I suggested that. She feels like she needs some exercise. I get the impression she's not much of a fan of standing around all evening, champagne glass in hand."

***

Madame St Romain stood on the little stage and with a knife, subtly tapped her champagne flute into the microphone. The room fell silent—such well-mannered people, the rich. She welcomed everyone, thanked her tirelessly hard working committee, thanked the sponsorship of the *Nicois-Massena Group*, in particular pointing out to everyone Chairman Albert Tarrant, and introduced the six featured painters to warm applause.

She spoke of their wonderful contribution to the cultural life of Nice, their dedication to their art, their genius in being able to realise in oils and water colours the rich tapestry of their imaginations.

A man placed an easel on the platform next to Madame St Romain. Another carried in a frame, covered in a white cloth, which he placed on it. Across the room, in a corner, I saw Louise closely watching, enjoying the proceedings.

Madame St Romain introduced each painter individually, and revealed their contribution to the evening's event. The level of applause rose from 'polite' and stopped short of 'overly enthusiastic' as each painting was revealed. After all the paintings were previewed, Antoinette announced, "My friends, we'll begin the auction in ten minutes."

I intended keeping my hands firmly in my pocket, for I remembered a time in my childhood, back in Australia, my father took me to a horse auction. I would have been ten or twelve. He told me to keep my hands in my pockets, and even though there were many flies around, I was not to brush them away; unless of course I wanted to inadvertently buy a racehorse for tens of thousands of dollars. And if I happened to, I would certainly be going without an ice cream at the end of the day.

The preview of the paintings to be auctioned began to reinforce my ideas for my *Mozi-Art* event. I now wished to talk with the painters present, catching them before they left. *No rush,* I thought. *They're artists and they won't be leaving until the free champagne has been drained.*

I looked about the room and pulled up short. Standing in the doorway, over by the *Nicois-Massena* banner, dressed as I had never seen her before, was Angelie Faivre. She didn't always appear as a farmer, for she'd been wearing fashionable blue jeans when I'd seen her last at Louise's Friday night dinner. Tonight, there was not a hint of blue jeans or the farmer from up on top of Eze.

She wore a tight fitting crimson mid length dress. Remy's boxing lessons, for the purpose of her fitness, were certainly having the desired effect. I noticed she had on makeup and lipstick. Tonight, any of her rough edges were well and truly smoothed over. It was one hell of an outfit to put on merely to drive Eloise home.

I searched the room. Eloise was nowhere to be seen. I hadn't recalled her leaving, though then again, my job was to vet the arrivals, not note the departures. I tried to remember whom she'd arrived with. I went back to the lectern to satisfy my curiosity.

By the time I maneuvered my way through the crowd, Angelie was no longer there by the banner. I consulted my list. Eloise had arrived with Paul Villan. I searched the room for him. He was chatting with Felicity Deschamps.

There's no accounting for some people's taste, I thought. *Why would one toss over Eloise for Felicity? Or had Eloise left early, not knowing Angelie was arriving for her?*

Angelie was now making her way through the room. Men parted for her to squeeze by, though their movement was not the sudden withdrawal Gabrielle Surmount had generated.

I crossed to Lautrelle Martin. "Can we have a quick word?" I took him aside and outlined my idea for *Mozi-Art*. He didn't say 'no'; he didn't say 'yes'. He did, however, agree to meet me on Tuesday.

I then followed up with the other featured artists in the room—Martin Beauchamps, Zelic Haberl, Heloise de Compte and Noel Fucheon. I avoided Gabrielle Surmount. They all treated my overture as Lautrelle had. *Is reservation and suspicion something inherent within artists?*

As I thanked Noel Fucheon for his interest in my idea, I heard behind me, "So, what disease do I have? Can't be the clap, the doctor cleared me of that, last week!"

I turned and placed both my hands over my privates. Gabrielle Surmount, wild red hair ablaze and reddish veins popping in her cheeks, guffawed. "I like you! You've a sense of humour!" My gesture had nothing to do with humour and a lot to do with self-preservation. "I hear you're after some special paintings."

I had to tell her. I couldn't insult her by saying she wasn't invited to contribute.

"Okay, I'll be there—Tuesday for lunch—*L'Opera Mozart*. I look forward to what you're planning. Give me a kiss, handsome." She flung her arms around me and planted a sloppy one on my lips.

I should have clenched my teeth. She slid her tongue in and wiggled it about. There are some men who'd be aroused by her doing that. Thankfully, I was still three lifetimes away from attaining that desire.

I found Louise and swapped my empty glass for a full one. I swallowed half the glass trying to wash down Gabrielle's marijuana-stained breath.

The auction began. Over to my left, the mayor was in deep conversation with Paul Villan. Pierre was chatting with Francine, the nameless redhead on his arm uninterested. Luigi was hovering, ready to move on anyone who stumbled too near his boss.

All were only half-paying attention to how much the paintings were fetching. I saw Albert Tarrant poke his finger in the air, Madame St Romaine point to him and wait for other bids, which weren't forthcoming. She clapped her hands, exclaimed, "Sold!" and everyone applauded. I guess Albert Tarrant would not be getting an ice cream on his way home!

I knocked back the remaining champagne. It was high quality—even so, it took me another glass to be finally rid of Gabrielle's kiss.

Once the auction was over, and an enormous amount of money had been pledged, the enthusiasm of congratulations heaped upon the buyers began to subside. Some people took it as their cue to drift off.

I said good night to those I knew and to those strangers who offered me a *bon soir*. I hoped they'd had a lovely evening. They all told me they had.

I noticed Angelie Faivre leave the restaurant, out through the kitchen. *Why not the front door?* I wondered. *Doesn't she wish to speak to me?*

Angelie was arm in arm with a man. *A man?* I peered closer. Angelie was not leaving with a man. She was leaving with the incognito Belinda Swann.

Chapter 6

Pierre Legrande, tailed by Big Luigi, approached me with the tall Eurasian model on his arm. I could have sworn the look in Luigi's eyes read: *How come Dougay gets to walk her home?* Being around six foot, her eyes were a little below my level and some distance above Pierre's. He introduced her and explained who she was. I said I'd been informed of all the details by his brother. He muttered something derogatory about the law finally being up to speed. Big Luigi scoffed.

Pierre left her with me. It was not an unpleasant experience to have her standing nearby, just hanging there. I smiled. She smiled back. What do you say to one of the most exotically beautiful women in the world? I asked her what country she was from. Her expression did not change.

She said to me in English, "I'm sorry, I do not speak French." It wasn't that she spoke English which set me back rather she spoke it with an Australian accent!

I could feel the smile growing over my face, like a child realising he'd woken on Christmas morning. She looked at me slightly puzzled. "What is it?"

"So, what part of Australia are you from, mate?" I asked in my broadest accent—the one Mary-Anne Walton could never understand.

She laughed out loud and fired back, "Melbourne, mate!"

"What's your footy team?"

"Richmond."

I breathed a sigh of relief. "Thank the Lord it's not Collingwood or Carlton."

She laughed. "And you?"

"I grew up in Sydney. So…"

"The Swans are my second team!"

"Marry me?" I asked in French, jokingly.

Louise was beside me. "What did you just say?" She asked with alarm, punching me on the upper arm. "Grow up!" She admonished. Sometimes young people are far too old and sensible for their own good.

"Ah, Louise, this is Sue-Lin Cambridge, an international model, here on the Riviera promoting swimwear and unfortunately, for you, she does not speak French."

"You remembered my name!" Sue-Lin exclaimed, surprised that she'd recognised it among my mouthful of French.

"Yes, mate," I said, unable to stop smiling at her. I turned my attention back to Louise. "We have to walk Sue-Lin home."

"Dougay, I came over to tell you that I'm not going home with you. Martin is here. He will walk me home."

Over from me Martin waved. I waved and smiled back warmly. I leant into Louise. "How'd he get in without an invitation?" I gave her an exaggerated quizzical raise of my eyebrow.

"I don't know," said Louise. "You were supposed to be on the door. Any riff-raff could have snuck in!"

"And they did!" I shot back, jokingly. Louise slapped me again on the arm. "Ow!" I said, faking hurt. "Take him and be careful walking home. There are idiots out there. Oh, did Raphael pay you?"

"Yes, good money, unlike you." Looking at Sue-Lin, Louise stood on tiptoes and made a show of kissing me on the cheek. "Goodnight, papa," she managed in English, with a cheeky smile, before taking my advice and Martin's arm.

"Ah, she's not my daughter, she's my flatmate, and my employee!" I don't think that sounded too convincing. I went on to explain to Sue-Lin that I'd need a few minutes to see if my job for the evening was over, and if it was okay, for me to leave. If truth be known, I really wanted Raphael to pay me as well.

I found him and he did. Louise was right. It was good money.

When I returned to Sue-Lin, Lautrelle Martin was speaking to her. "You're wasting your time, Lautrelle, she doesn't understand a word you're saying."

"That is of no concern to me! A lot of French women do not understand what I'm saying, though they are soon won over by my artistic skills." He waved *adieu,* after giving Sue-Lin his card, and stumbled out the door. She watched him go.

I guess the free champagne had run out. No, it hadn't. Gabrielle Surmount, once more with two glasses of the stuff, staggered over and tried to kiss me goodnight. She stumbled. I caught her with the aid of Sue-Lin's quick reflexes, and between the three of us, we managed not to spill a drop.

Gabrielle drained both glasses, handed me the empties and floated out the door into the darkness, calling back, "Tuesday! I will see you on Tuesday!"

"Believe it or not," I said, "I'm told she's a very talented artist." Sue-Lin did not reply, her eyes still looking after Gabrielle, concerned. "Also, the man who'd been talking to you."

"Yes, I saw his painting tonight—very impressive. I think he wanted me to pose for him. I tried to explain only in a bikini, not nude."

I didn't want to think of either image. I'm too young to suffer angina.

Sue-Lin handed me the card Lautrelle had given her. I pocketed it.

"I told him, some other time." She then asked, "What's that in French?"

"*Une autre fois.*"

Sue-Lin repeated it, until I nodded that she'd gotten her tongue correctly around its pronunciation.

I opened the restaurant's door, Sue-Lin easing by me. With her model's grace, she seemingly glided forward on air. By contrast, Gabrielle Surmount had managed to stumble safely away. There was no sprawled artist on the pavement outside.

"What hotel are you staying at, Madame?" I asked.

"Madame? Why so formal all of a sudden?"

"I've a very formal task at hand. There are serious expectations on me for your safe delivery."

"The Hotel Negresco."

Of course, I thought.

"It's very up-market. Not really my style, though I can tolerate the five-star establishment."

Tolerate? A luxury hotel? She has a sense of humour!

"Thank goodness, while on the Riviera, *Kanga Swimwear* is paying all my expenses."

"Kanga?"

"Yes, as in Kangaroo. They're an Australian company."

I nodded as if I'd heard of them. Fashionable swimwear? As if I would have!

"Their logo is a little kangaroo hopping on the side of your ass!" She laughed.

"Truly?" I asked.

"Yes!"

"Where is the kangaroo hopping on the G-strings?"

She laughed unreservedly and punched me playfully on the arm. What an angel!

"Yes," she reflected. "The Hotel Negresco. Sometimes I fall on my feet." I think she fell on her feet the moment her genetic combination emerged from her mother's womb and the doctor smacked her on her then Kanga-free ass.

We walked off. She paused and changing her train of thought, said, "I'm not a fan of champagne. I've hardly had a drink all night. I don't suppose you know a bar on the way, where we can sit for a while, away from the bullshit. Understand?"

"Oh yes, I understand only too well. They can take the girl out of Melbourne; however, not Melbourne out of the girl, eh?"

"Exactly. I could kill for a beer! So, any ideas?"

I looked at her as if I was about to divulge a state secret. I whispered, "Ever tasted slivovitz?"

***

Milos was closing up when we got to *Vlatava-Elbe.* He took one look at Sue-Lin and stopped turning the key in the lock. "For you, I am closed, but for her, I am open, twenty-four-seven."

"Inside or outside?" I asked Sue-Lin.

"There are no tables out here, which is a shame. The evening is quite mild."

"Milos? Any chance of a…"

Milos had two chairs in either hand, placing them next to us. "Dougay, get a table."

We sat around the table. Milos placed another two chairs beside us. He left and returned with a tray on which were four shot glasses and a bottle of slivovitz.

"Four?" I asked.

"Yes, Milovic is on his way!"

"How did he know I was here?"

Milos shrugged innocently, and for me the penny dropped. "Yes, I confess, I called him." Then he lowered his voice. "I tell him, get over here, if he wish to see most beautiful woman in world. Then I tell him, she with Dougay! He laugh and laugh."

At that moment, I heard Milovic come around the corner. He was still laughing! He stopped laughing when he drew near and saw the beauty of Sue-Lin emerge from the darkness.

Milovic shouted, "I'll need a double, Milos!"

All four of us sat around the table in the dark, lit only by a safety light inside the bar. I introduced Sue-Lin formally to them, explaining who she was and where she was from.

An hour later, after many questions from Milovic, answers from Sue-Lin, and laughter from all four of us, we bid goodnight; though I did not believe that it was a Czech custom, that upon meeting a beautiful woman for the first time, you had to kiss her three times when departing.

Still, Milos and Milovic insisted that it was the case, and that the tradition went back to the time Good King Wenceslas looked out on the feast of Stephen. Sue-Lin didn't object, and with good humour she let them have their childish fun.

On the way to her hotel, Sue-Lin and I swapped life stories. I told her how my parents were French and both dead.

She told me that her mother was an Australian-born Chinese, her father a fifth generation Irish-Australian and both were alive back home in Melbourne, where one day she intended retiring to—not specifically Richmond, rather Australia—after pulling the plug on the indecently financially rewarding life she was now living.

She said something about me being a nice guy, a down-to-Earth Aussie, and asked if she could keep in contact. She thought I could somehow become a point of reference for her, to help keep her feet firmly on the ground, while working in the crazy celebrity world of fashion. I gave her my email address and mobile number, though I told her I preferred the phone contact, because I didn't have a laptop or computer.

She suggested I should buy one. She thanked me several times for not fawning over her, for keeping my paws off her, and for not being false. I guess the beers were having an effect on her tongue.

It seemed as if we'd known each other for years. I knew it wasn't love or anything down that track, though I do confess 'comfortableness' was what I was feeling. I shook her hand at the entrance of *L'Hotel Negresco,* looking up into her eyes as she stood on the second white marble step, me on the pavement. The uniformed doorman studied me suspiciously.

Sue-Lin stepped down to my level and kissed me once on both cheeks saying, "In the French style." Then she laughed and kissed me deliberately three times on both cheeks, adding, "In the Czech style!"

I could have stayed there all night with her on the pavement corner of the hotel, her kissing me goodnight with the moonlit Mediterranean across from us, ignoring the doorman. I didn't. I watched that gorgeous creature turn away and enter the chandelier lit foyer. I held the moment. I then walked away knowing I'd never again see, in the flesh, such a vision.

***

I was lost in my thoughts of Sue-Lin, wondering why I felt so warm towards her, after such a short time, when up ahead a couple emerged from *Hotel Westminster*. They were Paul Villan and Felicity Deschamps. They'd obviously been drinking on after the art event.

I still found it unbelievable that he'd be interested in taking that woman to bed, because he didn't look drunk enough to be contemplating it.

Enough of them, I thought dismissively. *I have a memory of Sue-Lin to get back to.* I continued walking homewards, closing in on them from behind.

They didn't walk on. They stood outside the impressive hotel and waited, where a moment later they were joined from inside by a third person—Felicity's ex-husband, Pierre Deschamps, ex-deputy mayor of Nice!

What is going on here? I asked myself, stopping for a moment. *I thought they were estranged! Bitterly estranged!*

Felicity had employed the Private Investigator Jules St Croix, and indirectly me, to take photos of her husband in bed with that gorgeous blonde, Danielle Hubert, and then sent a photo to the paper, where the following Monday morning, it featured in a front-page spread! Her act of revenge ruined his political aspirations!

So why was she out having a drink with Paul Villan and her estranged husband? And why did her estranged husband just kiss her on the lips and squeeze her on the ass?

Paul Villan laughed at them, and caught up in their drunken bonhomie, they took no notice of me, as I stepped around them and walked by. I didn't walk quickly, because I didn't wish to draw attention to myself. They were now following me, and they began to speak, louder than normal, courtesy of the alcohol they'd been imbibing.

I picked up only snippets, all three voices overlapping.

"The more I think about it, the more I like it…A park! Why didn't you think of it before…? It dawned on me when I went there last weekend. The property developer in me says it's a real possibility…Does it need re-zoning…? It needs freeing up from government restrictions and then purchasing. We don't want anyone else sniffing this out…Can that woman be trusted…? There'll be a lot of noise from the crazy green left, when they find out…When they find out it'll be too late. By then, you'll be the new mayor…We can make our political move in a year's time…Exactly where is *Parc de L'Eco-Vallee*?"

They turned down a corner behind me, taking the remainder of the conversation with them.

***

When I got home, Louise was still up, sipping lemon flavoured hot water and watching late night television. I pointedly looked about the apartment for signs of Martin.

"He's not here, so there's no need for fatherly concern."

"I'm not concerned. It's your life, not mine."

She continued, wanting to explain. "We didn't have an argument. He only had time to walk me home. He has to finish an assignment."

"He sounds like a gentleman, who's not afraid of study."

Perhaps she was too shy to speak of him further, or she'd felt she'd offered me too much information, because she changed the subject. "You lost that beautiful model in the sea?"

"Something like that. I had to cast her adrift. She's not my type."

"Yes, I know your type. That woman at the Czech bar, the night we met, that American, the one who works for..." She paused and added, derogatively, "International producer Harold Kempenski." Then more positively, Louise said, "She's your type."

"Exactly!"

I went to bed. Louise had history, as a fourteen-year-old, with her mother and Kempenski. It was quite unsavoury, and I didn't wish to pursue it with her, because I didn't want her dwelling on it all night long.

Getting down deep under my covers, I was hoping to dream of Mary-Anne. If I dreamed of Sue-Lin instead, I wouldn't complain. I also wouldn't complain if I dreamt of Francine. Though if all three turned up in the same dream, and I had to stop them each from finding out about the other two, then that would be one hell of a pleasurable nightmare.

I could handle that, I reasoned. I wouldn't be able to handle the nightmare if Remy turned up sparring with Angelie in her chic crimson dress, high heels and boxing gloves!

"Are you awake?" Louise asked from her bedroom.

"No!" I called back. "I'm dreaming!"

Chapter 7

M'sieur Pom, as usual, was sitting behind his desk on his comfortable old chair in the foyer of our building, wearing a freshly ironed shirt. At this time of the day, his recently cut hair still had its dampness from his morning shower, his head buried in the morning newspaper.

"Is there anything in there about the art auction held for *The Society for the Advancement of Artistic Expression, Endeavour and Realisation on the Cote d'Azur?*" I asked, closing the elevator's iron doors. He looked up at me quizzically. Before he could question why, I added, "I was there last night."

"You?" He put down his newspaper, his curiosity aroused.

"Yes, I was the Maître d', in charge of the proceedings." I crossed to him. "I got to choose the best dressed man, the best dressed woman, and the best dressed miniature poodle dog carried in a hand bag."

"Have a nice day," he said to me, dismissively in English with a Gallic accented American twang. He lifted the paper to his eyes, covering his face once more.

"No, seriously, I was there."

M'sieur Pom dramatically turned over the pages of the newspaper until he found the society pictures. He snorted.

"Well, I never! Here you are in the background, looking lasciviously over this Asian model."

He had my interest now. I reached for the paper. He withheld it from my grasp, instead turning it around and showing me a photograph of Sue-Lin Cambridge. I was nowhere to be seen in the shot.

"Gotcha!" He laughed. I studied the other photographs on the page.

Francine stood in a quartet with her fiancé, the mayor, property developer Paul Villan, *Nicois Messena's* chairman, Albert Tarrant, and that first-class bitch Felicity Deschamps. If this photograph was an example of the company Francine had always dreamed of being a part of, she could keep it.

There was another photograph, a two shot of Francine and Albert Tarrant. They seemed comfortable together. *Do they know each other? If so, how well? Recently or from an earlier time?* Up until now, I hadn't been aware jealousy was a part of my genetic makeup.

That reporter, Mimi Benoit, hadn't lied when she gatecrashed, for she was certainly on duty last night. Her name was attached to the accompanying article, which according to M'sieur Pom was full of observations, anecdotes concerning those in attendance, and quotes from interviews conducted.

M'sieur Pom tapped a photograph. "They had a lot to say, though not about the art auction, only about themselves." He was indicating the young, gym-fit couple, with the cinema-spotlit teeth.

Antoinette St Romain featured in several of the other photographs, which wasn't surprising, considering it was after all her event. Clearly, the newspaper's photographic editor knew that if he wanted his team to get back in there next year, he had to keep the society's president happy.

The Legrande Brothers were not featured at all in the photographic spread, for they wouldn't see personal publicity as enhancing their lives in any way. I could hear them telling me, *Let others claim the spotlight, Dougay. I'm happy in the shadows!* However, they'd feel that way for opposing reasons. In the shadows, Pierre kept his head down; Raphael kept his eyes wide open.

Belinda Swann's disguise had been successful. There was neither picture, nor mention in the accompanying text of a 'Nick and Nora Charles'.

"When you're finished with that," I asked M'sieur Pom, "is there any chance of you cutting out the photograph of that Eurasian model, so I can have it, please?"

"When was I employed to acquire pictures of beautiful women for you?" Then he remembered. "Where's that magazine of Nice's bathing beauties I leant you last year?"

"Still upstairs. It was very useful; more useful than you can imagine." The magazine had featured a photograph of a model in a cream tiled shower, with a maroon border, which tied into my investigation at the time. It was at this basement location where Eloise had been abused, and Danielle had been murdered by Belinda Swann and her now dead husband, Calvin deMarko.

"I bet it was," he said, suggestively.

"That model in question," I began, tapping my finger gently on Sue-Lin's face, so as not to damage it, "is an Australian. Last night, I walked her home in the moonlight, and we told each other our life stories. We shared our hopes. And I have now become part of her dreams."

"What is that English word, all you Australians speak?"

"*Bullshit?*"

"Yes, that's it. *Bullshit!*"

Before he could carry on any further, I asked, "Where is *Parc de L'Eco-Vallee*?"

"Why do you ask?" M'sieur Pom has a relentless inquisitive nature. His devouring of the daily newspaper is not merely done to kill time; he actually loves studying the ins and outs of those who occupy his hometown. He was sure to know where the park was.

"I'm thinking of asking Madame Legrande to accompany me on a tram ride there today."

"You're planning on going there, and you don't know where it is?" He asked, incredulously.

"I only got in town a year ago."

"It feels a lot longer," he said, then winked, folding up his newspaper. "Why do you want to go there?"

"It was recommended to me," I lied.

"By whom?"

"A total stranger!"

He didn't believe me, and he was not letting me go, until I had offered him a reasonable answer. "Why do you want Madame Legrande to accompany you?"

"Are we in a television programme called *Twenty Questions?*"

He thought a moment. "You go in there and ask Madame Legrande, and I'll ask my wife, and we'll all go and have a picnic out there together."

I love how a simple idea of mine can suddenly be swept away and blown out of all proportion!

"Where's my photograph of that model?" I asked, not budging from in front of his desk.

From underneath, M'sieur Pom took a pair of scissors and carefully cut out the photograph of Sue-Lin Cambridge. He handed it to me, as if I'd just won gold in the fifteen hundred metres freestyle. I smiled in appreciation.

"Okay," I said, "we leave in fifty minutes."

***

From the tram stop, *Alsace-Lorraine*, we headed west, towards the airport, finally stopping after ten or eleven stops at *Grand Arenas*. I saw no huge football stadia there, only high-rise apartment buildings on all sides. A connecting green-line tram stopped, and we climbed aboard.

"*Bonjour*, Louis!" M'sieur Pom said, in the friendliest of voices.

"*Bonjour, bonjour*, Pom-Pom!" A very surprised passenger replied. "*Ca va?*"

Did M'sieur Pom know everyone in Nice?

The tram headed inland from the sea. Half a dozen stops on, M'sieur Pom said that it was time to alight. It had taken us about an hour to get to *Parc de L'Eco-Vallee*.

Leaving the exposed tram stop, which seemed to be out in the middle of nowhere, we walked back the way we'd come and immediately took a road off to our right. Down a short way was a horse-riding school; a man and woman with helmets on their heads, putting their respective mounts through manoeuvres. Opposite, a small car parking area was attached to the gated park. We entered through a turnstyle.

A sign read: 'Thank you for respecting this natural space'. It was my idea of a public park; it was not over managed. Grass grew where it wanted; a circular path meandered around where some gardener had randomly fashioned it; and planted palm trees sprung up, like Triffids in that sci-fi novel I'd read at school, happily for our sake, firmly rooted.

A couple of dogs played, their owners chatting and some horses stood in an adjacent yard, perhaps the stabling area for the riding school on the other side of the park's outer fence. The sign had been correct. It was all very natural. I looked to the hills in the distance. I could not believe that the thriving population of the Cote d'Azur was over there, a simple tram ride away.

We found a wooden picnic table and Madame Pom spread out a red and white checked tablecloth. Madame Legrande unpacked from her carry bag, pate and cheese. M'sieur Pom unwrapped the bread stick he'd been gently nursing all the way on the trams. I uncorked a bottle of red wine.

After we toasted each other's good health, M'sieur Pom explained how the palm trees had been brought in on a digger and individually planted into the patterns they now occupied. Madame Pom said that the whole area was managed by *Nice-Parcs, Jardins et Promenades* for everyone to enjoy. Madame Legrande said that it would be a real shame if Nice were ever to lose such a breathing space. What is it with old people and parks?

I knew why that property developer, Paul Villan, was so taken by the place. There seemed to be nothing here, nothing to knock down, nothing for people to get upset about losing.

After we'd eaten, I drifted off daydreaming.

"Moni Goumas," I heard Madame Legrande say.

"Yes," said M'sieur Pom, thankful that the correct name had been found to the question he must have asked.

"Was she Moni Flourent, at school?" Madame Pom asked.

"Yes. You remember, her family had money?"

"Yes. She always felt she was a little better than us. Well, better than me," qualified Madame Pom. "What became of her?"

I drifted off into my reverie once more. Better to leave the oldies reminiscing about people I've never met, than try to follow their conversation.

I was sprung from my reverie by Madame Legrande, declaring, "Dougay, don't you ever do that!"

"Do what?" I struggled to say, having missed the point of their story.

"Marry a woman, give her a beautiful daughter, then thirty-five years later, after stealing the family's inheritance, run off to Lyon or Paris or wherever, with some young tart."

I smiled at Madame Legrande and said mock-seriously, "Madame, you know my heart is only for you." The Poms laughed. "Though I have been warned by your two sons to keep my distance or…"

"Or what?" Madame Legrande asked, curiously.

"Or they'll weigh me down with pockets full of lead, and drag me behind a speedboat all the way to Africa."

"Rubbish," said Madame Legrande. "Neither of them know where Africa is. They both failed Geography at school."

The three oldies laughed.

Madame Legrande went on. "Moni Goumas, three years ago had to take a job. It was, for her, a very rude awakening."

"What did she end up doing?" The ever-inquisitive M'sieur Pom asked.

"Nursing sick children. The only qualification she has is possession of a kind heart."

"That must have been a big come down and loss of face for her," commented Madame Pom.

"Yes," agreed Madame Legrande. "And there but for the grace of God…"

The other two nodded, understanding the short distance between their apartments on Avenue Auber and the poorhouse. Though I knew the Poms would hit Struggle Street well before Madame Legrande would.

"Did her daughter do okay in life?" M'sieur Pom asked, always keen on knowing who was getting ahead and who was falling behind.

It was time to drift off again, though I did manage to hear Madame Legrande say, "Her daughter, Avril, actually works for *Parcs Nice*…"

Sometime later, Madame Legrande woke me and we all walked several times around the park for about an hour, before we took the return trams home. I was pleased my initial wariness at M'sieur Pom's suggestion had proved fruitless. It had been an exceedingly enjoyable afternoon.

***

That evening I went to clean up at *L'Opera Mozart* and asked Louise if she could prepare a luncheon tomorrow for six guests and me. I handed her fifty euro to buy the food. There were no customers in the cafe.

"I'm going home early, Louise. Have you your key?"

"Always, Dougay."

I dried my hands and dramatically tossed down the tea towel. "Finished!" I declared.

Louise carried over three dirty pans and dropped them into the emptied sink. I groaned.

***

Finally, I left *L'Opera Mozart* after stacking the pans and putting away the remaining dishes and cutlery. Louise had gone off to meet up with Martin somewhere, so from the base of the stairs I called out, *"Bon nuit*, Claude!" He called back, his voice muffled from behind his closed door up top.

I felt like a walk before going directly home, so I headed for a lashing of the cool night's sea breeze. As I approached the Mediterranean, I stopped walking and quickly eased into a closed shop's doorway. Two men walked by in front of me, coming from the street on my left. *What are those two clowns doing here in Nice?*

They were the policemen, who'd given me a hard time after I'd been bashed and dumped in a garbage dump. They'd been out to arrest me, having been tipped off that there was a sachet of cocaine up my ass. However, by the time those two lazy oafs had found me, I'd discovered the suppository and tossed it into the tip.

Thankfully, now, they passed by me without noticing. I tossed up whether to tail them or not. I guess M'sieur Pom's sense of curiosity was beginning to rub off on me. They walked with a purpose, neither saying a word to the other, their eyes fixed straight ahead. After a block, I realised how foolish I was behaving, and gave up the 'chase'.

I crossed over Promenade des Anglais at the pedestrian crossing and stood looking across the intersection to *L'Hotel Negresco*. In my mind's eye, I saw myself bid farewell to Sue-Lin Cambridge; I saw her go inside; and I saw myself walk off distracted.

I wondered how someone like me could ordinarily meet someone like her, as equals. If it wasn't for that task of walking her home, I'd have never come across her, for she was like one of those yachts moored in Cannes harbour—finely crafted, beautifully attired and ultimately unattainable.

Why was I thinking of Sue-Lin like this? *Summer is coming, Dougay, and Mary-Anne will be returning. Get your head together.*

I sucked in the night's sea air and walked home keeping an eye out for those visiting policemen.

***

The six artists were all on time. The offer of free food and wine has that effect on the artistic sensibility. I poured seven glasses of wine from two bottles, and we raised our glasses and clinked. It appeared as if a toast was being made, though only I knew as to what.

I sat at the other end of the table, as far as possible from Gabrielle Surmount. She would need the arms of an overdeveloped orangutan to reach my nether region from down there.

Louise brought out the platter she'd prepared. I admired how my fifty euro had been turned into such an appealing and appetising meal. My flatmate sure had a wonderful talent. We all ate and drank.

After their second glass of wine, I began my spiel, as I feared if I waited much longer their attentive brain cells would be irreparably damaged.

"I'm interested in holding an art event, here, in the back room of the cafe. As you can see the cafe is called *L'Opera Mozart*. I'd like to exhibit paintings of Mozart; however, with a twist. I'd like them to be humorous, irreverent, satiric, all with an overriding sense of fun. I'm planning on calling the event *Mozi-Art*."

"1.0," added Louise, from behind me.

I turned, looking at her thinking, *where did that come from?* "Yes," I said, "*Mozi-Art 1.0*." It just seemed to roll off the tongue.

"This will be the first," explained Louise.

I looked back up at her. *Whose idea is this?*

Louise went on. "Dougay is hoping that with its success, it will become an annual event, and part of Nice's artistic and social calendar. I'll let Dougay explain the details for you." She turned and walked inside. I could have smacked her bum! (In a fatherly way, of course.)

"Ah, so," I stammered, trying to reconnect my thoughts, "is four weeks long enough in which to paint a painting? I know nothing about art. I don't even know why I like what I like." The artists exchanged scornful glances. How many times had they heard this ignorant line of praise from those they'd sought commissions or sponsorships?

"I'd like to hold the opening on the first Sunday evening in April, mid spring. Invite people; rather like that event at *Le Grande Nice*."

During my spiel, the six had made no sound, no comment of approval or disapproval. I took their silence to mean they weren't interested. If I failed to engage them at this moment, I never would. I ploughed on.

"I'd exhibit the paintings for four weeks." There was still no comment from them. I played my remaining card. "There'd be a prize—money!"

Lautrelle spoke. "Why a prize? Why do you think we artists wish to compete against each other? I respect the work of every artist seated here. It is an insult to make us compete! You arts administrators, the world over, are a disgrace!"

He stood to go. The others began moving their chairs out from the table.

"Wait!" I shouted. They stopped and stared, the pressure of their eyes on me. And then, as is often the case, a snap judgement from left field spewed forth. "What if I commissioned you?"

Momentarily held in their various stages of rising, the artists, as one, slowly sat.

Noel Fucheon, the precisely mannered, grey bearded one of the collection, asked rationally, "Would we have total control over our work?"

"Apart from it being about Mozart, and it being satirical or humorous, then yes, you would have." I am no artist. I intended leaving all the detail to those who are.

Noel Fucheon went on. "Four weeks in which to deliver the painting, when would the deadline be?"

"The Wednesday before," I said, blindly thinking aloud. "It gives me time to hang them." I'd never hung an artwork before, so I was now making this up as I went along.

Zelic Haberl continued, "That's not long, but it's only satire. I suppose one could whip up a couple of splotches of ridicule." He focused on Gabrielle and said sarcastically, "I'm sure you could splosh something together, Gabi."

Gabrielle leant forward and quietly asked, "Your mother, Zelic, is she still having sex with dogs?"

"There's no need for rudeness, bitch!" Zelic stood and left without offering me a word of thanks for lunch! From across the street, he turned and shouted an expletive at Gabi, which was lost beneath a truck's horn. Gabi tossed her head back and laughed, matching the truck.

And then there were five.

"You'd have them here on display for four weeks afterwards?" Martin Beauchamps asked, the most ordinary looking of the group, who'd from the first time I'd met him, struck me more as an accountant than artist.

Gabrielle spoke, "If he buys them, Martin, he can display them for as long as he likes. He could even hang them up his ass if he wanted to."

Martin Beauchamps gave Gabrielle a withering look.

Heloise de Compte said, "I'm afraid neither competition, nor commission, appeals to me. I'm in Paris from Friday. Baron Moncur is missing my company once more."

"I don't know what you see in that old lecherous flea bag," said Gabrielle, sticking an unlit cigarette in her mouth.

Heloise bristled. "You said it yourself, darling. He looks at me lecherously." There was no love lost between these two women.

"What? Lecherously searching your pubic hair for fleas?" Gabrielle again laughed, uproarishly.

"I do not have to sit and listen to your foul-mouthed denigrations!" Heloise de Compte thanked me for lunch, wished me well with my project, and walked off towards the sea.

And then there were four.

Gabrielle lit her cigarette, inhaled deeply, and blew smoke over the rest of us! "Heloise is far too sensitive to be a real artist," she derided. "She's too uptight. Word is she's never once slept with any of her male models."

I was beginning to have had enough of Gabrielle Surmount destroying my idea before it even got off the ground. I leant across towards her saying, "Whereas, you do with all your models!"

She looked at me, surprised. "Of course; however, before I paint them. How do you think they get the job?" She laughed again, beginning to shake. "Do you, Dougay, wish to pose for me?" Was there no way, short of murder, of silencing this woman?

Martin Beauchamps apologised. "I have a commission, which I'm currently working on, and therefore, I'll be unable to contribute. I wish you well." He shook my hand, bid goodbye to the others, hoping their future projects were successful and disappeared down the street.

And then there were three.

I began to feel impending doom. Three? The walls of the backroom would look very barren if there were only three paintings to hang. That would be one painting per wall! That is, if these remaining three artists agreed to contribute anything at all. It was time to take charge of the meeting. I'd had enough of treating artists with kid gloves.

"Two and a half thousand euro each—one painting only, delivered by 6pm on the Wednesday before. Whatever you submit, I own. Take it, or leave it. That's my first and final offer."

The artists sensed the change in my attitude. They did a quick mental calculation as to the price of bread, cheese, pate, meat, alcohol and rent, multiplied by four weeks. They then took into consideration the fact that it was only a 'humorous' painting that was required, not a masterpiece to be displayed for eternity.

Simultaneously they said, "Okay!"

We shook hands and all four of us drained another two bottles of red.

***

That night in bed, I did my own mental calculation, through the haze of the afternoon's red wine's cloud. *3 x 2,500 euro = 7,500 euro!* What was I thinking?

Seven and half grand? There's no way Claude would come in as a partner on *Mozi-Art 1.0*. He hated every crazy idea I'd ever came up with!

I lay, open eyed, staring at the ceiling. From where could I borrow the money? Who did I know who had seven and half grand?

Pierre Legrande? No, I had no intention of getting into bed with the devil.

Seven and a half grand! Madame Legrande? No, I had no intention of getting into bed with the devil's mother, even though she was sweet and lovable and I trusted her. What if I couldn't repay it? She'd never forgive me!

Seven and half grand! Remy? No! Far too many numbers would be needed to be calculated and retained in the head, as he'd never allow anything to be entered on a spreadsheet.

Seven and half grand! Francine? I wondered what Francine was doing tonight. Was she ever going to miss me?

Snap out of it! This is serious! Seven and a half grand!

I was going to have to sell my first diamond.

Chapter 8

I left my apartment, and rather than wait for the elevator, I walked down the stairs. Naturally, the elevator passed me going up. As I approached the fourth floor, a man and a woman, about my age, came out of the rear apartment, the one belonging to Monsieur Degas.

"It's far too big for him," said the man. "Ever since Maman died, he's been lost in there."

"You sound like my husband," said the woman. "But you know papa, he will not leave!"

"If we could convince him to go to a retirement home, we could sell the apartment immediately."

"Yes," said the woman, "and you could pay off your gambling debts."

They stopped talking as they heard my footsteps approaching from the floor above.

"*Bonjour*," I said, cheerily, making out I hadn't heard.

"*Bonjour*," they muttered, lacking friendliness.

I was approaching M'sieur Pom in the foyer, when I suddenly stopped and let out a groan. I turned around and climbed back up the six flights. I passed Monsieur Degas' son and daughter descending in the elevator.

Before Louise had moved in, I used to leave my phone on the small dining table. Now, as the living space was shared, I'd moved its location to the set of drawers by my bed. I was not yet in the habit of always remembering it was there. I opened my apartment door.

"You're back early," Louise said, looking up from her coffee.

"Forgot my phone!" I went into my bedroom and pocketed it. As I left the apartment, I commented to her, "I hope the remainder of the day is going to improve."

This time I waited for the elevator. It arrived and I rode it down. *My day is improving,* I thought as the floors slid by. Walking towards M'sieur Pom a second time, he commented, "I thought you'd just left."

"Ha-ha!" I was trying to think of something witty to offer as a rejoinder when my mobile rang. It was Jules St Croix, the private detective.

"What are you doing?" He asked. "Got anything on today? Want to make some money?"

"How much are you willing to pay?" I asked, and knowing it would be too good to be true, added, "Seven and half thousand?"

"It's too early for jokes," he reprimanded. "Can you get over here by eleven this morning? We'll be finished by two."

"Yes, sure, I've nothing on."

"And I'll possibly need you tomorrow as well. I'll deduce that after we finish up today. Mind you, I'm hoping I can string it out a bit."

Jules was not a man who strove for immediately spectacular results. He was a plodder, rather than a sprinter.

He charged by the day, so if a case could be solved in twenty-four hours, he preferred to solve it in forty-eight or more.

I hung up and went to have my morning coffee at *L'Opera Mozart*. Claude was happily wiping down a table. I told him of the outcome of yesterday's meeting with the artists. Before he could complain about anything, I said, "I'm paying!"

"You?" He questioned, surprised. He stopped wiping down the table. "You're offering commissions?"

"That's right!"

"Why not offer a prize?"

"The artists don't like competing with each other."

"You're concerned with artistic sensibility?"

I didn't answer. I had no idea if I was or wasn't.

"Let me get this straight. You're paying artists to create paintings to hang on the wall of the backroom, so you can big note yourself as a patron of the arts? Where are you finding the money?"

As I knew he'd ask, I'd prepared my answer. "From my Italian aunt, remember her? She is the one who came up with the loan, so I could buy my five percent in this high-class café!"

***

I knocked over-dramatically on the door of Jules' office on Rue Alfred Mortier, over near the Museum of Modern and Contemporary Art. I shuddered as I walked by the pile of files in his tiny outer office. I was sure there were more stacked on the floor than last time I'd been there.

"When are you hiring a secretary who understands how to file?" I called out.

There was no reply. Behind his desk, he leant forward, appearing guilty, turning down the face of a framed photograph he had on the desk in front of him.

"What's that there, you're not wanting me to see?"

"I've trained you too well," he replied.

"Trained?" I scoffed. "Is that what they call it nowadays?"

He contemplated showing me. After a moment, he sheepishly passed the picture across his desk.

"Jules!" I exclaimed, "This is…"

"Yes, I know. I couldn't help myself. She had such a fabulous ass. And that cheeky *fleur de lis* is almost winking at me."

"She's dead, Jules," I said, solemnly.

"Yes, I know. It's my only weakness."

I did not believe that.

The framed picture was an enlarged copy of one of several hastily taken photographs Jules had shot of Danielle Hubert in bed with the ex-deputy mayor, Deschamps. However, it was not the famous one—the one splattered across the front page of the newspaper, as that one had not shown Danielle's tattoo, and therefore no link to *Milady* and Pierre Legrande.

Jules had been selective in handing over the photographs to his client. Fully aware of repercussions, Jules, like Danielle, knew how to keep his head down.

Tapping the photograph, I said, "I bumped into him the other night."

"Who? Pierre Deschamps?"

"Yes. He was out drinking with his ex-wife."

"That bitch, Felicity?"

"Yes."

"Rubbish!" He dismissed, scornfully.

"And he kissed her on the lips!"

"Did she slap his face?"

"No. She responded, willingly."

"Rubbish!"

"And then he took hold of a large lump of her ass and gave it a squeeze!"

"Rubbish! Rubbish! Rubbish!"

I let that echo around the room until it died its natural death. "I thought you said they were estranged, that she wanted to take him to the cleaners, as punishment for leaving her."

"I did. That's true! I told you about her." Then he looked cheekily at me. "Remember? I said you could jump her bones and I'd take the photographs."

I was not going to continue to play his childish games. I had far more self-dignity than that.

"I've always wondered, Jules. Why did Felicity Deschamps call you to take the photos?"

"I'm a top grade Private-Eye!"

I ignored that. "She knew where her husband would be! Who paid top dollar to have Danielle go down on him? The husband or the wife? Who told Danielle to leave the door unlocked so we could get in so easily?"

"Who are you, the public prosecutor?"

"Don't you question what really went on that day?"

"No, and you shouldn't either." He looked seriously at me. "I do not know anything."

I stared back with my best 'I don't believe a word you're saying' look.

"Okay, okay, that bitch Felicity Deschamps called me to take the photos. You know that, I told you. She set it all up and now the case is closed."

Something about the way he said that led me to believe the case may be closed; however, it hadn't been finalised. Again, he noted my look.

Whispering, he said, "That woman will not settle her account."

"She hasn't paid you? After all this time?"

"Exactly!"

"You want me to go around there and break her legs?" I asked in a mock-heavy gangster voice.

I don't think Jules was in the mood for humour. He said without irony, "Dougay, here in France, we don't live in a third-rate American movie. Anyway, why are you asking me all these questions? That blonde belonged to your best friend, Pierre Legrande!"

"He's not my best friend." I leant in. "Jules, why, Jules, Felicity and Deschamps—why are they so secretly buddy-buddy once again?"

"I don't know," he answered honestly. "The least I know about her, the better. How could I possibly know what they get up to?"

"All this kissing and ass squeezing happened in the presence of Paul Villan."

"Paul Villan?" Jules echoed, sharply. "Felicity Deschamps and Paul Villan? You know all the questionable types. How long have you lived here? Have you met any people, apart from me, worth knowing?"

He leant back in his chair and offered, seriously, "Dougay, you know me; keep your head down, that's my motto."

"Yes, and I have a lot of that motto in me as well." I pushed my interest in the Deschamps to one side, though I got the impression Jules hadn't. He was thinking of something. I suppose he was putting those three names together and striving for a connection. I broke his thought process. "So, what's happening today?"

"A husband thinks his wife may be cheating on him."

"Is this all you do—hop from one bedroom to another?"

"It's an honest living." I don't think he recognised the irony in what he'd said.

"If there's a savage dog involved, you're on your own."

***

We pulled up in Jules' car at the rear of a public-type building opposite to the entrance of its underground car park. Painted in a non-offensive grey, the building was a late twentieth century combination of glass, aluminium window frames and concrete prefabricated walls bolted together.

The three-storey rectangular cuboid had probably looked attractive on the plans; however, builders can sure stuff up an architect's vision. Or they can realise that limited vision to perfection.

"Does the husband or the wife work here?" I asked, only half interested.

"The wife." He consulted his hastily scrawled note. "Madame Petain."

"What makes him think she's having an affair in the middle of the day?" I asked, beginning to concentrate on the task at hand, wishing to have a clearer picture of what potential trouble, or embarrassment, lay ahead.

"Not generally in the middle of the day, but specifically over lunch," he made a point of clarifying. "Apparently, the husband's found some cash in the wife's bed-side drawer."

"And he suspects what, that she's screwing office workers in the broom cupboard for fifteen euro a pop?"

"Fifteen euro?" Jules reprimanded. "You have such a poor opinion of French women, Dougay."

"Quite the contrary, Jules. I have an enormously high opinion of French women. But, not of the tales you weave around them."

"Here," he said, handing me a car registration number, scrawled on a torn off piece of paper. There is nothing high-tech about Jules. "Go down there into the car park, walk around and see if she's at work today. If you can't find her car, then we can assume she's snuck out for a bit of pokey-pokey."

I looked at him. "Pokey-pokey?"

"Dougay, don't you understand the subtleties of the French language as well as you'd like to believe?"

I shook my head at his carry-on, and climbed out of the car. Walking down into the darkness of the car park, I stopped, waiting for my eyes to adjust. When they had, I wandered around as instructed. I found her car parked in the far corner. I turned around to go back to Jules.

"Great!" I exclaimed. There was CCTV in the car park. I hugged the shadows on the way back to Jules' car.

"Is she there?" He asked, as I climbed into the passenger seat.

"Yes."

"Okay, let's go home. We'll come back tomorrow."

"That's it? That's all?"

"As I said, the husband suspects his wife is having it off with someone during her lunch break." He glanced at his wristwatch. "Lunch is nearly over. We'll come back tomorrow a bit earlier, in case she heads out because she's feeling particularly," he paused, "hungry!"

"Will the time it has taken for this wasted exercise be billed to the husband?" I asked.

Jules laughed slyly. "Dougay, private enterprise is a wonderfully creative capitalistic concept."

***

I phoned Remy and asked for another favour. He met me outside my bank and escorted me away down the street. He had no idea what I was intending to do and I wasn't about to tell him. However, once again, I breathed a lot easier knowing he was there, walking beside me.

It was late afternoon, when I lent carefully against the door of *Lefbvre and Massenet, Jewellers*. I eased it open, as if it were as delicate as one of the diamonds inside the pouch I had in my pocket. A tinkle of a tiny bell rang overhead. A well-dressed woman behind the counter looked up and asked, "May I help you, Monsieur?"

"I'd like to look at engagement rings, please." I glanced behind to Remy, and then back at the woman. "We've decided at last to get married!"

Remy uttered a guttural sound that bore no resemblance to the French language and stumbled back, his eyes widening in horror. I laughed, "Sorry, Madame, my little joke."

The woman looked at Remy and asked me, "Do you think your friend needs a glass of water?"

"No, Madame. He'll be fine once he recovers from the shock. I've never mentioned how I truly feel about him."

"Enough!" Remy croaked, as the woman and I both shared a laugh at his expense.

I calmed and became serious. "Yes, Madame, you may certainly help me. I have a letter of introduction to Monsieur Massenet."

"May I see it, please?" She held out her hand. I gave her the letter in Audric's handwriting. As she read it, a smile came to her face. "He was such a lovely man."

"He still is," I said, lightly.

She looked up at me. "Why, yes, of course. I believe he's moved to Paris. I hope he'll be happy there, because there wasn't much happiness for him here. Far too many memories."

The woman went into the back room. After a short while, a little grey-haired man, with matching goatee, appeared.

"I am very pleased to meet you, Monsieur Roberre. Monsieur Lefbvre told me all about you. I have been expecting you. Though when, I had no idea. I believe you have brought sunshine once again into his life."

"Oh, perhaps I only opened the door to allow it in."

"Whatever, Monsieur, it was commendable of you. Please, come through to my office."

I thanked Remy for escorting me and asked if he'd like to sit and wait. He looked suspiciously at me, before indicating that he would. I went around the counter and followed the jeweller into the back room.

The woman was already waiting for us, seated. Monsieur Massenet sat behind his desk and I sat next to the woman.

"Now," he began, "how may I be of service?"

I showed him the certificates of authority and ownership, which Audric had left me. He studied them, muttering to himself as he read. After a moment, he looked up to me. "You are a very fortunate man, Monsieur Roberre."

"Yes, Monsieur Massenet, I believe I am." I cleared my throat. "I'm a little short of cash, not much, but even so; I was wondering if I should sell these as a whole or individually?"

I pulled open the drawstring on the small pouch. The jeweller reached in and selected a diamond at random. Into his left eye, he inserted a loupe. After a while studying the jewel, he took out a small note pad. He wrote down a figure. He showed it to me as he said, "Individually."

I nodded.

"May I have the pouch, please?" He asked.

I handed it to him. He carefully emptied out the remaining nine diamonds. He individually inspected them. He wrote again on the note pad. He showed me the figure, saying, "Collectively."

I know nothing about wheeling and dealing, nor the value of diamonds, so innocently I asked, "Is that your best offer, Monsieur?"

The precisely groomed jeweller studied me for a moment. Monsieur Lefbvre said that you'd drive a hard bargain, and when you did, I was to give you the best possible price. It is fortunate for you that only yesterday, I had an enquiry from a woman in Monaco, to fashion for her a diamond studded necklace of a sentimental chain left to her by her maiden aunt.

"These diamonds of yours will be perfect for that. Your timing could not have been, like these diamonds, more perfect."

I wondered for a moment if he was attempting to delude me, the woman seated next to me or himself. Still, whatever inflated price he'd offer, I'd be grateful for, and not concerned if he passed on the mark-up to the woman in Monaco.

Monsieur Massenet wrote once more on his note pad. He lifted it slowly into my line of vision. I noted the amount written there. It was inflated! Up until now, only women had been capable of taking my breath away.

I indicated the ten diamonds were his, and Monsieur Massenet nodded to Madame. On her laptop, she transferred an enormous amount of money into my bank account.

I took Remy for a celebratory coffee. To this day, he thinks I sold a locket from the estate of my Italian aunt.

***

I'd washed up in the cafe, locked the front door and walked home in the dark with Louise. I made my world-famous toasted cheese and tomato sandwiches for dinner, refraining from offering Louise *Spicey-Ricey*. Even though she gladly ate them, Louise still made a point of explaining they were the reason I was never to go into *L'Opera Mozart's* kitchen and use her stove!

We watched some news bulletins on television.

"Why do you look at it so fiercely?" She asked. "You concentrate so hard on everything you see."

"I'm trying to match the words across the bottom of the screen with what is being said."

"Why?"

"I'm trying to teach myself to read."

"You can't read?" She asked, surprised.

"English. I read English."

"Oh, yes, of course, I remember. At Sunday's art auction, you asked me to read aloud that banner. I wondered why."

"Well, now you know," I said simply. One day I was going to have to try and make a more formal effort to learn.

I washed up the dishes and wiped down the bench top. The laminex around the sink was starting to come away. *One day*, I reminded myself, *get a new kitchen!*

Louise bid me, *"Bon nuit,"* and wandered off to her bedroom.

I lay on my bed in my old man's flannelette striped pyjamas, the ones I wore in winter. In summer, I used to sleep in a kangaroo T-shirt. Francine souvenired that. I wished she'd return it, like right now!

My mobile rang. I recognised the caller ID. "Eloise?" I asked, tentatively. I had no idea why she'd be calling me at this time of night. "Are you okay?"

"Hey, that you, Dougay?" She asked with a nervous excitement. There was a pause.

"Yes!" I waited for her to go on. "It's me!"

"You're breaking up." Her voice sounded distant, muffled, like she was in a car or on a bus. "It's a very poor connection.

"Wait! I'll go out into Place Mozart." I climbed out of bed. "The signal should be better out there."

"Hello, hello, that you, Dougay?"

"Hang up!" I stressed with restraint, not wishing to wake Louise. "I'll call you back."

I stepped into my pair of ratty old slippers and put my goat herder's jacket over the striped pyjamas. If Sue-Lin could see me now, she'd have never asked for my email address.

The elevator was on the ground floor. I didn't wish to wake anyone, so I hastily tip toed down the stairs and crossed the foyer. The light under Madame Legrande's door was out and M'sieur Pom had retired to bed.

Across from Rue Beethoven, I entered Place Mozart and phoned back Eloise. The call rang out. I walked further towards the centre to be more in the open, away from the line of the surrounding buildings. I redialled Eloise's number. It rang out a second time.

Are you okay, Eloise? Why are you calling me so late at night?

I headed back to my apartment block, hoping nothing could be amiss with her. Off to my right, a dark car was leaving Rue Beethoven. In front of me, there was a large lump on the footpath. My heart stopped. "Oh no," I said out loud. "*Déjà vu.*"

I quickly crossed to the lifeless form, wrapped in a dark blanket and whispered, "Eloise?" I carefully rolled the body over. The blanket fell away to reveal the dirty cream and grey clothing of a young man.

It was not a young man. It was a battered Belinda Swann. She muttered in her breathless American, "Don't call the cops. Don't call the cops."

Chapter 9

By the time I'd managed to get her up onto my hip and gently drag her arm over my shoulder, M'sieur Pom had the front door open. I struggled carefully with her towards him.

"I heard the car drive off," he said. "It left too slowly to be anything other than suspicious."

Belinda Swann hung off me like a large rag doll; the stuffing knocked out of her, her breathing irregular. I carefully eased her down past M'sieur Pom's desk. Behind me, he looked out onto the footpath. He went out and bundled up the blanket. He came back in and locked the front door.

I stopped halfway between his desk and the elevator, waiting for him to catch me up. He indicated the blanket and whispered, "Will you be needing this?"

I shook my head. He stowed it beneath his desk, then walked past me to the elevator, opening the iron gates. He too knew the routine.

"Before a young woman, now a young man," he quietly began, cheekily. "Don't you know which way to swing?" I was holding Belinda Swann in my arms, her face away from him.

"M'sieur Pom, I know you're an avid reader of the news; however, I don't believe you're an avid peddler of gossip, so therefore, do I have your vow of silence?"

"Dougay, I was joking. I do not care if one minute you rescue a woman or the next a man."

"Do I have your word?" I quietly stressed.

M'sieur Pom sensed my seriousness. "Yes, *mon ami*, of course." I turned Belinda's face to him. "*Mon Dieu!*" He had recognised her.

"Exactly. *Mon Dieu!*" I whispered, "come on, ride up with her and I'll take the stairs, just like last time."

A light came on under Madame Legrande's door. "It's just me, Madame," I whispered. "I can't sleep." The light went out.

M'sieur Pom entered the elevator and I carefully passed over Belinda Swann, gently propping her against his body and quietly closing the iron gates.

When the elevator stopped at the landing in front of my apartment, M'sieur Pom managed to hold open the iron door, keeping the elevator there, waiting, until I climbed the final two flights. I took hold of Belinda Swann and M'sieur Pom opened my apartment. I lifted her into my arms and carried her in, as once I'd carried in Eloise Pittard.

"Is Louise awake?" M'sieur Pom whispered.

"I don't know," I whispered back. I carefully laid Belinda Swann on the sofa and then stood up, stretching.

"Yes, I'm awake," said Louise, emerging from her bedroom, tying a dressing gown around herself. "Who have you got there?"

I looked at the two of them standing, staring back at me, waiting for an explanation. "All answers in the morning," I said. "Okay? Okay?" They both nodded. "It's past your bed time, isn't it, M'sieur Pom?"

He smiled, taking the hint. He bid us, "*Bon nuit*," knowing he'd hear all about it come daylight.

Closing the door behind him, I said to Louise, "Help me get her undressed and cleaned up."

"Her?" She queried. I began untying Belinda Swann's black patent leather shoes.

"You seem to know what you're doing," Louise commented, standing back observing my every move.

"Only too well." After I had the shoes and socks off, I held Belinda's shoulders, easing her slightly forward from the waist. "The vest, Louise." Belinda groaned as Louise eased it off around her and over her shoulders.

"Nice clothes," Louise appraised, feeling the material. "Expensive."

"Only, if like you and me, one is poor. These clothes are not expensive for her."

"Her?" She queried again, not yet realising.

"Take a closer look." I gently placed my index finger under Belinda Swann's chin and raised her face to Louise. It took a moment for Louise to register.

"Yes," I said, confirming Louise's disbelief. "She's famous, eh? So, not a word to anyone. Belinda Swann is not here."

Together, Louise and I continued to undress the actress, as carefully as we could. Even so, it was painful for Belinda.

"Dougay, doesn't this bother you?" Louise asked with concern.

"Having women beaten and dumped on the footpath outside my apartment does; undressing them, doesn't. It is the only thing in life I am qualified to do."

Louise suppressed a laugh, breaking the tension for both of us.

I eased my arm under Belinda's knees, and the other under her shoulders, carefully lifting her from the sofa. I carried her towards the bathroom.

Louise commented, "If only your friends could see you now."

"Yes, the old Bondi gang would erect a beach statue dedicated to me—*Dougay and the Mermaid*."

I carefully lowered Belinda's legs and held her upright in the shower. Louise reached across and turned on a tap. The gush of water hit my arm and shoulder. I pulled back from the stream of cold water, cursing. Louise adjusted the taps, trying to suppress a laugh, followed by a mirthfully false apology.

"Louise, while I hold her upright, wash away that blood from her face."

Louise did. "She's a mess."

"She sure is. Someone knew what they were doing."

After cleaning her face, Louise began to carefully wipe down Belinda's arms and torso, while I continued to hold her floppily upright.

"This bit won't wash off," Louise said curiously. "I never knew she had a birth mark."

"She hasn't," I said. "Go lightly, it's a bruise."

Louise turned off the shower and found a towel. She began to carefully pat Belinda dry. She then held her upright, while I found an old shirt to wrap her in. I deliberately did not give her the one I'd wrapped around Eloise.

I carried Belinda back to the sofa and lay her down, dragging my duvet from the bed and laying it across her. Tonight, I'd be sleeping wrapped in my overcoat with thick socks on my feet.

As Louise began to drape Belinda's cream trousers over the back of a dining chair, a wallet fell from a pocket. Searching the other pockets, Louise found a turned off mobile and a USB stick, a piece of red ribbon tied to it. I took them all from her and placed them on the dining table.

"Bedtime," I said to Louise. "It's late. We've done all we can."

"Shouldn't someone sit up with her?"

"I don't think that will be necessary. If tradition is anything to go by, Belinda Swann will be gone by sun up."

***

She was. All that remained was my crumpled shirt on the sofa and the USB stick with the attached red ribbon on the table. Perhaps, it wasn't hers. I stuck a pin through the ribbon and fixed it on my notice board, next to my hand written note: 'Buy Milk!' and the newspaper's photograph of Sue-Lin Cambridge.

It had taken me a long time to fall asleep last night; not because I was cold, lying there in the beautiful overcoat Francine had bought me in Milan, rather because I lay in the darkness thinking, thoughts tumbling over and over. Even when I was sure I had some things making sense, I still could not let them rest.

Once or twice in the past I'd felt *déjà vu*. However, what had happened tonight was not *déjà vu*. There was no sense of the accidental involved in any of this. It had been deliberate; deliberately planned and deliberately executed.

Eloise Pittard had called me, getting me downstairs with that phony faulty phone call. Had she wanted me to find Belinda dumped, as she had been similarly dumped outside my apartment block? Had Belinda been deliberately left there knowing I'd take her in and clean her up?

I believed it had been a staged re-enactment. The question nagging at me was for which one of us? A re-enactment for Belinda Swann? Or a re-enactment for me?

Eloise could not have done this by herself. It would take two people to get Belinda out of that car. So who was her accomplice? The more I thought, the more I realised the event was not a re-enactment for me. All this had been staged and executed for Belinda Swann. So, who could've inflicted the punishment?

Eloise worked for Pierre Legrande. Could it have been Pierre Legrande who'd done this—the final act of retribution for what had happened to his two girls? Was this his vengeance on Belinda Swann for her involvement in Eloise's assault and Danielle's death?

He'd had Belinda's husband, Calvin deMarko, dealt with, albeit from a distance. Could the extra muscle Eloise have needed, been supplied by Big Luigi?

The last time I saw Belinda, she was leaving the Art Event, Sunday evening, arm in arm with Angelie Faivre, the lover of Eloise. More logically it was Angelie who'd done this. Though, could Pierre have used Angelie as bait to lure Belinda from that art auction?

He'd deliberately stayed behind in the restaurant having that meeting with the manager of the *Water Babies* stores he owned. Was that meeting not legitimate? Was it, as M'sieur Pom called, a 'smoke screen'? I was once again thinking of Pierre being behind the assault, though I soon countered that by believing it wasn't his style, for he'd been in Europe when Calvin deMarko had been killed by that truck in America!

At some time during the night, I said out loud, "Forget Pierre Legrande!"

Could Angelie have been the one to beat up Belinda Swann? Angelie had been taking boxing lessons from Remy. I could almost hear her sweet voice convincing him.

"Remy, baby, I'd love to learn to box, only for fitness reasons, truly, I don't like pumping iron. I want to remain lady-like." I remember Remy falling for it; he'd told me enough that he was sparring with her.

"Teach me to box, Remy, and I'm sure that one day you could convince me to have a relationship with a real man like you." Sometimes, I'm just too cynical.

If it had been Angelie, how long ago had she planned her revenge? How long had she been prepared to wait for Belinda Swann to return to Nice? She knew in time Belinda would. Angelie was a lesbian and Antoinette St Romain of course, they knew each other!

Angelie would have known that Belinda was coming here for Antoinette's birthday. The society dame had even told me, a male stranger, that she had.

On Sunday evening, I had seen Eloise talking on her mobile. I now felt she'd been calling Angelie, telling her Belinda Swann was at the art event. Angelie then dressed up to the nines and drove down from Eze, and weaved her way past everyone, with eyes only for *Nora Charles*!

I'd been impressed by the sight of Angelie in that crimson dress, so I was sure Belinda Swann had been as well. Bait. And the fish had nibbled.

Did I care? No, I didn't. Belinda had viciously assaulted Eloise and been a participant in the murder of Danielle Hubert. I was not going to confront Angelie and I knew Belinda Swann wasn't going to say anything to the cops. She was here incognito, and incognito was how she was planning on staying.

Belinda is alive, so leave well enough alone, Dougay. As far as I was concerned, the matter was ancient history, never to be revisited. I should have known you can never be certain about anything.

Chapter 10

The stakeout with Jules was dragging on. Madame Petain didn't go to work on Friday, and being employed by the government, she didn't go to work over the weekend. Jules said for me to be ready Monday, as he was planning on busting the case wide open. The only thing he had a chance of busting wide open were his trousers from too much sitting down, eating croissants and cakes.

L'Opera Mozart hadn't yet re-opened regularly on a Saturday night, so I went to *Vlatava-Elbe* for a night with Milovic and his mates on the slivovitz and dark Kozel beer.

When I arrived, Milovic and Milos carried on about me taking Sue-Lin there for a late-night drink, and then carried on about the fact I walked her home. I soon stopped their carry on.

"Milovic, Milos," I said, "Sue-Lin was very pleased to meet you both." The two men smiled, pleased they'd impressed the international model. Ulna, Milovic's wife, pricked up her ears.

"She was delighted you introduced her to the ancient Czech custom of kissing a departing 'beautiful', no, 'extremely beautiful' woman, three times."

"Three times?" Ulna interrogated. "Milovic, you kissed an 'extremely beautiful' woman good bye, three times?"

My two Czech mates didn't mention Sue-Lin again.

After I knocked back my second shot, Milovic leant in and whispered, "Guess who I drove to the airport this afternoon?"

"I have no idea."

"That gay guy who 'hired' my car that time I had to clean out the rear seat." Milovic worked as a chauffeur for a limousine hire company. "Remember?"

"Oh, him," I said, pretending to be uninterested. I knew he meant the unpleasant Beau Andrews.

"And," he paused for effect, "Belinda Swann."

"Is she back in town?" I asked, innocently.

"Back in town, and once again in the back seat of my limousine. She was travelling incog…how do you say that word in English?"

"No idea, but in Latin you say, *incognito.*"

"Yes, incognito." He ran his tongue around the word, remembering it for next time, though I doubted he'd be having another incognito femme-fatale in his limo quite like Belinda Swann again. "She didn't look too healthy. I know those film stars all hide behind dark glasses, but she must have been on a heavy drinking binge, because I think she'd had a fall.

"Her face was cut and bruised. Apart from that, she looked okay outside, expensive clothes, but inside? She was carrying something in there." He touched his lower abdomen. "Her companion had to help her in and out of the car."

I knew what Milovic meant about how Belinda would be feeling inside. No matter what you covered yourself in, nothing could hide the way you carried yourself. I should know. I remembered the time I'd been bashed and dumped on that roadside garbage tip, on the outskirts of Aix-en-Provence.

"I collected her from a private address, not a hotel, nor that film producer's boat moored in Cannes. That's how I know she was here *incognito*! As the Latins say." He'd learnt the new word and was pleased with himself. "She's been staying with that rich society dame—sister of the mayor."

"Oh, her," I said, and wishing to lighten the conversation added, "the woman your wife regularly joins for cards and dancing?" Milovic laughed and explained to Ulna, who turned up her lips and opened her eyes in fake alarm. She spoke rapidly to her husband.

Milovic translated. "My wife says she has no desire to mingle in that sort of society, nor with those sorts of women."

Ulna spoke again. Milovic again translated for me. "However, if I continue staying out late at night, drinking with you, she may change her mind!" Ulna laughed and slapped me on the knee!

I went for a leak. Slivovitz and beer have that effect on me. On the rear wall of the bar, out back by the toilets, I noticed a window up high had been replaced by a piece of board. On the way back, I asked Milos, "Why'd you board up the back window?"

"No choice. Some assholes smashed it, broke in, stole money."

"When?"

"Thursday night. I go bank Friday. They took all week's money. *Bastardi!*"

"Are you going to leave it like that?" I asked, thinking there might be a small repair job in it for me.

"No, I have cousin. He fixes. Delayed. Wife in hospital. First child."

Around midnight, I paid my bill and bid Milovic and Ulna *bon nuit*. On the way back to my apartment, I deliberately avoided staggering past Francine's apartment, though I confess, I toyed with the idea for quite a while.

***

On Monday, half an hour before the lunch break, Jules pulled up in the same spot outside the public building he'd parked in last week. "Run down and see if she's at work today, will you?"

I didn't run, I walked. When working for such a high-class private investigator as Jules St Croix, it's best not to draw attention to yourself. I stayed in the shadows, crossing to where Madame Petain's car had been parked last time. It was there again. I skulked back in the dark, avoiding the CCTV camera, sitting once more beside Jules.

"Her car's there," I reported.

"Go inside and see if she's in the office," he said. "She may have left on foot."

"You want me to ask for her at the front desk?" I asked, unbelievingly.

"Yes."

"What's her name? What does she do in there? What if they ask me what I want with her?"

"Gee, you're difficult to work with. Madame Petain. Didn't I tell you last week?"

"Last week, when was that?" I asked, stirring him.

Jules looked at me with a withering look and uttered, "Why do I bother?"

"Alright, give me a piece of paper and a pen."

Jules stretched over me and opened his glove box. I wrote on the paper and gave him back his pen.

"What have you written?" He asked, eager to know.

"My calling card."

I crossed the street and entered the building through the automatic sliding glass doors. At the reception desk, I asked the woman seated behind it, "Is Madame Petain in, please?"

The receptionist reached for the phone. She raised it to her ear then stopped. "What is it about, Monsieur? Madame Petain is a very busy woman, as I'm sure you realise."

"I have this appointment," I said, handing her the note I'd written.

She studied it. She put down the phone. "Monsieur," she began pointing to the note, "today is Monday. This appointment you have is for tomorrow."

I took it back feigning surprise. "Sorry!" I exclaimed and smacked my forehead in realisation. I turned and disappeared out the door. Climbing into Jules' car, I said, "She's at work."

"Well done," conceded Jules. "Anything else?"

"Yes, her shoe size is six." I laughed. Jules didn't.

We sat in the car waiting for lunch to roll around. Jules reminisced about playing rugby when he was a teenager in school. I let him.

When he took breath, I said, "Jules, I've been thinking about that time we first worked together, the time I wrestled that mongrel dog."

"Again? Get over it!" Then his eyes widened in fear. "You're not going to ask for Worker's Compensation, are you?"

"No, you paid me for that job, right? And now you say Felicity Deschamps hasn't paid you. Do you want me to return the money?"

"No! No, *mon ami*. Unlike her, I am an honourable person."

We sat and waited some more. Nothing remotely interesting was happening on the street. After a while, I tapped Jules' arm, waking him.

"Jules, have you wondered that possibly Madame Petain goes to lunch on foot, out the front door?"

"Merde! Go around the front and follow her if she leaves that way."

I started getting out of the car. I turned back to him. "What does she look like?"

"*Merde! Merde! Merde!*" He exclaimed, hitting the steering wheel with the palm of his hand.

"Didn't you bring a photograph of her?"

***

We returned on Tuesday with a photograph. At this rate, the husband was going to need a bank loan to pay Jules' account. Sitting in the car outside the building, in the same spot as yesterday, I studied her image before handing it back to him.

"She's okay, isn't she," Jules said. "I wouldn't kick her out of bed on a cold windy night to make her go close the banging window shutter."

"Jules, you love your work too much."

We sat waiting, and waiting and waiting. I was dreaming of Mary-Anne. I was riding a wave on Bondi beach. I was photographing Sue-Lin in a swimsuit for a magazine spread. I jumped when my mobile rang. It was Francine.

"I have a job for you. Are you interested?" She asked.

"One minute," I said, and climbed out of Jules' car onto the footpath for privacy. "Go ahead."

"Friday evening, I need you to go to a hotel in Cannes and pick up…you are free on Friday evening?"

"Yes," I replied.

"All night?" She asked. I hesitated. "No, don't think like that. I'm an engaged woman now. The job requires some time on your part. You are to go to this woman, pick up the document and bring it back to me. I'll be in my office until eight. I sign it, you return it to her, and then you can go home."

"Okay; however, can't she just come to you? Makes it a lot simpler."

"That woman and I cannot be seen in the same room together."

"Okay, sorry, I understand. Details?"

"6.30 pm; *Hotel Abrial*. It's east of the train station, along the railway line. At the desk ask for Madame Charlottenburg. I'll reimburse you your train fare."

"Are you well? How are you feel…" She'd hung up.

It was a choice of standing on the footpath pretending I was talking to Francine or sitting back in the car with Jules. I chose to stay on the footpath, my phone to my ear, listening to nothing.

Jules called out, "Time to go around the front! I'm not paying you to while away hours on the telephone!" I put my mobile away and set off.

After about fifteen minutes, I recognised Madame Petain. I'd never tell him so; however, Jules was correct, she was not hard on the eyes. She was laughing with three other women from the office. I took out my mobile and whispered, "I have her in my sights."

"Don't lose her, and don't get sprung!"

There was nothing special about the quartet, just work friends heading out to lunch. All were dressed similarly. All were of a similar age. One was taller than the others.

The four women had no idea I was even in Nice, let alone on the street behind them. They gesticulated, they laughed, they gossiped, they loved life. I followed them to a bistro. They had lunch.

There they gesticulated, they conversed, they laughed, they gossiped, they enjoyed eating. After forty-five minutes, they walked back to the office.

I climbed in the car next to Jules. "Nothing. She only had salad. She's either looking after her figure or she's a vegetarian."

"That's it?" He asked. "Nothing else to report?"

"She's left-handed."

***

On Wednesday, Madame Petain stayed in and probably ate at her desk.

"The husband might be paranoid," I said. "This woman is not having an affair at lunch."

"As long as he's paying, we're watching." In that short statement, Jules had summed up his entire business philosophy.

We were back in place on Thursday. I once again checked that her car was in the car park. As I walked down the all too familiar ramp, she drove by me, her car braking at the roadway before heading out. I ran back up to Jules.

"She's off!" I shouted, jumping in the front seat, waking him from his slumber. "*Allez! Allez!* Jules, the red car, up ahead!" Jules headed off, keeping a safe distance.

She drove west from the city, up beyond *Grand Arenas*, heading inland. She pulled up next to a dark car, in the car park of the *Parc de L'Eco-Vallee*.

"I was only here last week," I said. "That building she works in, Jules, what is it?" I needed to feed a growing curiosity.

"City Administrative Centre, why?"

I didn't say a word, I just felt strange about this. I felt a lot stranger, when out of the dark car a man climbed, and sat in the passenger seat of the red car next to Madame Petain.

"*Mon Dieu!*" Jules exclaimed. "That's Paul Villan!"

"Yes," I said. "How do you know him?"

"We go back a long way." There was no tenderness in his voice, and he left it at that.

We sat and waited. Paul Villan and Madame Petain stayed seated in the red car.

"Get your camera out, Jules. I'll go for a little walk over there. If they start kissing and cuddling, click away."

"Are you now telling me my job?"

I climbed out of Jules' car and walked off through the turnstyle into the park, pretending I was interested in the palm trees. I couldn't see clearly into the red car, for there were too many shadows on its windscreen. However, I could see enough to tell me that they weren't kissing and cuddling. They were sitting side by side, more like brother and sister than passionate lovers.

After a while, Paul Villan opened his door and climbed out. Then Madame Petain got out and joined him.

I was surprised, shocked even. I looked at the crumpled photograph I had of Madame Petain. I looked up at the woman with Paul Villan. I looked back at the photograph. This woman was not Madame Petain, rather one of the friends she'd had lunch with the other day, the tall one.

I walked back to Jules, who was now out of the car. "Forget it, Jules. It's not Madame Petain. It's one of her lunch pals." And then one of those wonderful left field thoughts I have, hit me.

"Follow them into the park. Take photographs. In particular, take her photograph, Jules," I added, excitedly. "Get a close up."

"Why? If it's not her, why bother? I'm not prepared to waste film."

"Film? Your camera is digital!" I held his arm. "Jules, for once trust me. It'll be needed for archival purposes," I lied.

To his credit, the years of him being a snoop came to the fore. They didn't know he was there, as he tracked them in his best nonchalant manner, keeping out of sight behind the palm trees.

Paul Villan walked his companion slowly around the park, pointing to imaginary things, making grand gestures with his arms. He was explaining; she was imagining. They returned to their respective cars and drove off.

"Did you get a close up of the woman?" I asked, sitting back in Jules' car.

"Of course, I'm a professional."

"Good," I said. "Send me the best close up you have of her."

"Why? You thinking of asking her out on a date?"

***

On Friday at lunch, the real Madame Petain went again to the local bistro with her workmates. The tall woman, who'd borrowed her car, was with them once again.

"Jules, Madame Petain is not having a lunchtime affair," I said, deliberately. "The money in her bedside drawer might simply be savings she's putting aside for a considerable purchase. Maybe even a surprise birthday gift for her overly suspicious husband. Tell him his suspicions are ruining his marriage."

"You're right, Dougay. Here." Jules knew the case had fizzled out to nothing yesterday, for he handed me an envelope of cash he'd prepared overnight. "*Merci, mon ami.*"

Walking from Jules' office, things I'd seen at *Parc de L'Eco-Vallee* were gnawing at me. Once home, I stopped off downstairs, knocking on Madame Legrande's door.

"I was just heading out. Care to join me?" She asked. "I'm only going to sit in the sunshine in Place Mozart for an hour."

"Of course." I escorted her out of the building.

"Where are you two off to?" The inquisitive M'sieur Pom asked.

"The Chapel of Love; we're getting hitched," I quipped. He scoffed at my lame joke.

Madame and I sat on our favourite bench. We'd sat here so often that someday, in the far, far distant future, the city administrators should screw onto the bench a plaque with our names on it, as testament to our existence.

"Madame, I'd like you to look at something, please."

"I've seen it, Dougay. It didn't impress me then, and it won't impress me now!"

"Madame! You are a devil." She laughed. I took out my mobile phone and found the close-up photograph Jules had sent me of the woman with Paul Villan.

"Where did you get that?" She asked, surprised.

"Can't tell you. Do you know her?"

"Of course. That's Avril Goumas. She's the daughter of an old school friend of mine. I was only talking of her last week! You were there! Where did you get that photograph?"

I ignored the question. "Where does she work? Do you know?"

"She's the personal assistant to one of those government types, the one who administers where we were the other day—parks. She's number two, below the managing director in the authority which looks after all the parks in Nice."

Chapter 11

"Oh!" I exclaimed. "Holy *merde*!" I cursed.

I leapt from my Princess Grace's pink duvet onto my feet, shattering my reverie. I'd been thinking of how and when I'd go about replacing my old kitchen. Dreams would have to wait. I had an errand to run.

It was around 4pm, and I had to be in Cannes, at that hotel to pick up the documents for Francine from Madame Charlottenburg. I rushed from the apartment. I stopped at the elevator. I returned inside. I'd forgotten my phone!

In the short time, it took to get back to the elevator, it was heading to the ground floor. I hurried down the stairs and passed it, as it ascended with Monsieur Degas inside. We gave each other a wave.

I took the train to Cannes. The flood of tourists, which swamped it in summer, was still several months away, so I didn't have to queue long at a tickct machine. That was never a pressing problem, as I can stand in a line and let my mind drift, keeping at bay any build-up of possible annoyance.

In summer, the pressing problem was once on board finding a piece of pole in the carriage to hang onto, while the train lurched into and out of each station rattling westwards.

In the carriage today, there was only a mother and child—
a loud, whining, complaining brat. When his mother ignored
him, he started running from seat to seat, pretending he was
being chased, screaming out as if being set upon in a back
alley by a demented axe murderer.

In my Australian accented English, I deliberately asked
his mother if she spoke my mother tongue. She derisively
shook her head. I turned to the kid and whispered curtly, in
my broadest Aussie accent, "Sit down, you little deadshit!"

On Cannes platform, I tapped into my mobile directions
for *L'Hotel Abrial.* I headed in the direction Francine had said,
to a market, its paraphernalia being packed away into many
vans parked higgledy-piggledy around the square. I picked
my way through and around them, further down small streets
until I came upon a major road and the railway line.

Ahead, to my right, was a vertical sign for the hotel, above
a luxury used car showroom. If Madame Charlottenburg
required privacy, then she'd found a suitable place for it.

I pushed open the door and crossed the small well-
maintained foyer to the reception desk. There a very friendly
young woman asked if she could be of assistance. A man at
the computer seated behind her, turned and smiled up at me.

I asked for Madame Charlottenburg.

While the young woman consulted her files, I strolled
away into a small dining area, sparsely furnished with simple
white tables and chairs. A very tiny bar was tucked into a
corner and ahead of me up some steps was an undercover
sitting area. I decided that when I had collected what I needed
from Madame Charlottenburg, I'd return here and sit a while
nursing a beer, before heading back to the railway station.

The young woman called out, "Sir!" I crossed to her. "Madame Charlottenburg is in Room 203." She indicated the elevator and light grey marble stairway off the foyer. "On the second floor, Monsieur."

I thanked her and walked up.

I knocked on the door. A female arm came out and dragged me inside. Francine kissed me and pushed the door closed behind my back.

"So," I mumbled, trying to speak around the mouthful of kisses she was giving me, "I assume there are no documents." She laughed and started unbuckling my belt. I was now laughing along with her.

Out the corner of my eye, I noted Madame Charlottenburg had ordered two delivered pizzas and a six-pack of beer. She kept kissing and turning me, as if we were in some slow-motion Fred and Ginger routine. We fell on the already down-turned bed. The pizza and beer would have to wait. We didn't get near it for about twelve minutes.

"Twelve minutes?" Francine questioned, slumping back, breathing heavily. "You're losing your stamina."

"I've missed you." I tried to make out it was a lie, by carrying on with false bravado, though she knew I had, and I knew she had as well, for I'd heard her whisper to herself, as she rolled off me, "God, I needed that!"

Lying stretched out on our sides we held each other, both sliding into our thoughts of the other. Her eyes were on the ceiling, mine were jammed beneath her armpit.

"Francine," I began, "when I'm with you, I lose sense of time and awareness of anyone else living in the world."

Her eyes came from the ceiling to me. "That sounds rehearsed."

"Perhaps. I've been thinking about it a lot, and it needed to be said."

"Anything else you need to say?" She asked.

"Yes, how's your life of celibacy going?"

She laughed and punched my arm.

We dined on cold pizza and warm beer. I didn't mind, I was with Francine.

It was around 2am when I woke. I desperately needed a leak and a sip of water. I was bent over the bathroom sink, water running into my cupped hand, my lips having just started to get wet, when I felt Francine's arms go around me. Keeping me in that bent position, I felt her face turn sideways and rest on the back of my shoulders.

For a moment, she held me without moving. She then held me tighter as her body began to shake a little, crying.

Back in bed, I told her I'd always be there for her. I wasn't lying. I meant every word. "I know what you need to do, and I have accepted that," I said, trying to convince myself more than her.

"Shh," was all she replied.

I fell asleep.

In the morning, I found a hand written note next to my phone. I showered and dressed, and as I went down in the elevator to the hotel's foyer, I hoped she'd paid the hotel bill. She had.

I left *L'Hotel Abrial* without having that beer I'd promised myself in the cute corner bar. Ah well, I had other memories of the place to take with me!

On the train back to Nice, I couldn't get an image of Francine out of my head. She was sitting cross-legged on the bed, eating a slice of pizza with one hand, while drinking her bottle of beer with the other. She was enjoying it so much, that for a moment, I thought she may have been part Australian!

Her jet-black hair was out and hanging long and ruffled after lovemaking, her makeup blurred. She seemed vulnerable, and of course, highly adorable. She wore my old Australian T-shirt, her bare legs invitingly open. The old man kangaroo, hopping across her breasts, was smiling at me.

***

I walked from Gare de Nice homewards. The last time I'd walked this way, I was a mess of contradictory thoughts and obsessions, wondering what to do with Audric's diamonds. Now, I only had the one sensation—I was consumed by a feeling of numbness. Not a physical numbness from last night's activities, rather a spiritual one. Francine has a knack of pounding my heart into joyous submission, and then leaving it to recover of its own accord.

I opened the door and the strong smell of disinfectant smacked me in the nostrils. Louise was cleaning the apartment!

"I hope she was worth it!" Louise said, cheerily, as I closed the door. "I have been slaving away in here all night and day, while you're out there, drinking and carousing with wild women!"

Little did she know!

"I hope you're joking," I managed to say, looking distractedly around the room. I hadn't noticed until now, though I guess over the past week or so, Louise had been tidying things up. The living area was getting a definite feminine touch. There was even a cushion on the sofa!

"Don't bother with the kitchen," I said, wishing to ease her burden. "I'm thinking of tearing it out soon and putting in a new one." I could have eased her burden a lot quicker by helping her clean.

"Really?" She asked, stopping her scrubbing, propping back on her haunches. "Will you be getting it through Remy or do you want the stove to work properly?"

"I've been thinking about spending a bit more money and buying brand new appliances. My aunt in Italy has come through for me." I don't think I'm ever going to stop lying to my friends.

I sat at the dining table, Louise joining me, asking eagerly, "So, what kind of a new stove can I have?"

"You have?"

"Well, you don't call what you do in the kitchen 'cooking', do you?"

"Give me time to think about it," I said, sounding a lot like Claude.

There was a small vase on the table with six bright yellow flowers in it. "Are these daffodils?" I asked, taking a sniff.

"Yes, with orange centres! I bought them last evening; the evening you didn't come home."

"Sorry, mother," I said, giving her a wide-eyed stare.

"They're beautiful, aren't they?"

I nodded and wondered what else had become 'beautiful' in my apartment, this past week. I glanced inside my bedroom. Thankfully, its mess was still in place.

"What's the occasion?" I asked, impressed with what I'd seen. "Why all the cleaning?"

"Well, some people may, one day, drop in for a chat."

"People? Or one person—Martin, in particular?" She smiled coyly. "Does he have a proper job yet, or will I be supporting him as well?"

"No!" She exclaimed. I'd touched a nerve.

"Sorry, I was joking," I admitted, back-pedalling. "You've kissed him then, since my last update?"

She didn't say a word, instead nodding her head from side to side, as if to say, 'maybe'.

"Is that a 'yes'?"

She paused then admitted shyly, "Yes."

"Has he got bad breath?"

She slapped out at me. I pulled back. She didn't connect. I poked out my tongue. She laughed with me.

"So, what's his job?" I already knew the answer. I just wanted Louise to open up about Martin.

"Who are you, my father?"

"Step father, fairy godfather; well, does he have a job?"

"Yes, I told you, though I got that slightly wrong. He's not a lawyer. He was helping out in a law firm. That was a part time job until he graduated. He's a schoolteacher. He will be when he graduates after the summer."

"Cup of coffee, Louise?" I asked, as I headed into the kitchen to boil the kettle.

"Yes, please."

When I'd made it, Louise tossed aside her cleaning rag and we sat at the table.

"Dougay, do you think Belinda Swann will be okay? She was very knocked about. Who'd do such a thing? And to such a famous person?"

"I don't know, Louise, though I think she'll be okay."

"How do you know that?"

"Remember my Czech mate, Milovic?"

Louise nodded, "Yes."

"He happened to drive her to the airport in his limousine. So yes, she'll be okay."

I took out the note Francine had left me. "Louise, I found this lying in the street," I lied. "Can you read it for me, please?" She took it.

I love you, though I cannot love you. I have to appear to love another. If I don't then one day, I will die unfulfilled, never having satisfied myself. I will always try to look out for you, as I know you have promised to do for me. F.

I pinned the note to my noticeboard, next to the red-ribboned USB stick, and Sue-Lin's photo. My noticeboard was getting crowded. *I must be accumulating a life here in Nice.*

Louise watched my every move. "If you found that note in the street, why do you bother keeping it?" I didn't reply. "And why do you bother pinning it up where you can see it every time you enter the kitchen?"

***

During the early morning, I woke. Realising, I said to myself, "March sixteen." Thinking of the note I'd received from Francine, I muttered ironically, "What a gift. Happy forty-second birthday, Dougay."

***

Remy stepped back and dropped his arms. "That's it," he said, exasperated. "Enough is enough!" He stared at me. "You're not even trying."

"Yes, I am," I objected, unconvincingly.

"Your head's not in this."

I mockingly bounced my head from side to side, imitating the technique he'd taught me when first we'd began these sessions. "I'm getting a new kitchen. That might be the reason I can't concentrate."

"And I'm getting a new sparring partner!" He hit me on the shoulder. The blow stung me into action. "I danced around him and laid pulled punches over his body." He began to laugh. "It's like fighting a mosquito!" He shouted.

I'll show you! I foolishly thought. I let him have one to the chest. It knocked him back a couple of paces. He looked at me. I waited for his retaliation. It didn't come. I was now seriously worried, because he simply started taking off his gloves.

"Your foot work's improving, at last," he commented. I should have been on guard, because I rarely receive a positive word from Remy. He added, "Must be the quality of your teacher."

I scoffed. As I undid my gloves, Remy squatted quickly and hit me bare knuckled on the ass. He didn't pull the punch. He knew it wasn't going to do any damage down there, other than make me walk with a limp for twenty minutes.

"Ow!" I screamed, over reacting.

"A new kitchen, eh?"

"Yes," I replied through gritted teeth, rubbing my ass. "A 'brand new' one," I stipulated, now unconcerned about letting him down easily. "Not used. Nor fallen off the back of a truck," I added, pointedly catching his eye.

He wasn't insulted. I should have known, as nothing seems to faze Remy. "Ever thought of getting an induction cook top over a fan forced oven?" He asked. "Also, a double-sided sink?"

"My kitchen's not large enough."

"They come in half sizes, designed for modern apartment living, with the draining tray moveable, so you store it over the second sink." Had Remy swallowed a manufacturer's brochure?

"I hadn't thought of that," I confessed.

"Well, start thinking. And a new fridge, upside down or traditional?"

"I've still got a lot of decisions to make." I put my sweaty head into a towel.

After a while sitting like that, Remy carefully eased back a fold of my towel and peered closely at me, saying, "I have a cousin's wife, whose sister's husband just happens to work in white goods."

***

I knocked on the outer office door of Francine's legal practise. The young receptionist, whose name I vowed one day to learn, looked up and smiled in recognition. Francine recognising my footsteps, opened her office door and ushered me inside.

Before she could ask, say, or do anything, I said, "This is business, strictly business."

"You sound like me," she admitted. "Like mistress, like pupil."

"Mistress?" I posed, smiling at her.

"Moving on. How can I be of assistance?" The lawyer in her was well and truly back in place, Madame Charlottenburg well and truly back in Cannes.

"I'd like you to draw up a contract for me, three in fact, that say I'll buy a painting for two and a half thousand euro. Leave blank the painter's name and the title of the work. I can fill that in." I went on to explain everything about *Mozi-Art 1.0*.

"Sounds fun," she said, genuinely interested. "I'll try to be there. I hope there's a spare moment in my fiancé's diary." Did she say that with a tinge of regret?

She made a note of the details. On the way out, Francine whispered, "Did you get my note?" I said I did. "I meant every word."

***

Submission day arrived—the Wednesday before the grand *Mozi-Art1.0* opening.

I went to *L'Opera Mozart* early. I shouldn't have bothered. I hung around all day waiting, every hour my level of worry rising. What if no paintings materialised? There's not much history of galleries exhibiting 'invisible art', and I didn't want to start the trend.

I should have paid those painters a deposit, to somehow guarantee they'd submit. *How reliable are artists one has only briefly met?*

145

After 4 pm, a small delivery truck arrived. My artists were very reliable. My concerns vanished.

"*L'Opera Mozart*?" The driver asked. I pointed to the name above the cafe and nodded. I guess deliverymen are paid to drive, not read. I helped carry in three individually wrapped paintings. As I rested the third one against the far wall in the backroom, the driver presented me with a document.

"The artists got together and hired the one delivery truck," he informed me. "They said that it would save you money."

"Me?"

"They said you'd pay!"

I'd not realised I'd be paying for the delivery! I guess this was an example of not dotting all the Is nor crossing all the Ts. I should have put something concerning that into the fine print on their contracts. Not that I had given them their contracts yet.

"In the arts," I began, handing over the cash, "the only people who seem to make money are the people who hire out the truck."

He said nothing. He'd probably heard people bitching to him about 'cost' all his working life. He took my cash, and I signed his clipboard. He ripped off the white sheet, keeping the pink and blue ones for himself.

I waved the truck off, as the three artists, together, turned the corner. They'd come for their money! I could tell, they had that artistic look of avarice in their eyes.

On the contracts, they filled in their names, the title of their work, signed and I counter-signed. I paid them, handing them a duplicate of the contract. Everything was now legal. I owned three unseen paintings.

My father's advice rang in my ears. *Never buy sight unseen!* "Sorry, Dad," I whispered, under my breath.

I wished the three artists well, hoping to see them on Sunday evening. They said they'd be here, with friends.

"Only three?" Louise asked, standing in the archway, staring at the wrapped paintings propped against the barren wall in the cafe's back room.

"Afraid so," I admitted. "It's a start. We could hang them far apart, keep the crowd moving about the room."

She thought about that, while I sat and looked at the blank walls, wondering in which order the three different sizes would be best arranged.

"I liked what that art woman did at that society auction," Louise said. "She made everyone focus on revealing one painting at a time. So, on our big night, we should have the paintings covered, and then unveil them individually. Inject a bit of 'theatre' into the night, some drama."

I thought about this. "Louise, I think you've saved the day!"

"Hadn't you better unwrap the coverings, to see what those artists have painted for you?"

I found a sharp knife and carefully sliced through the wrappings. Louise and I sat back, staring at the three individual art works, lost for words to describe what we were going to hang.

***

Saturday afternoon, Remy and I sparred. He was losing his touch. He didn't once try to trick me into falling for an unseen blow to the kidneys. Maybe that was the trick—do nothing, and have me worried, waiting all session for the trick to occur.

After the sweat out and wash in the sink, I said, "Hey! You've got a laptop."

"I've had the laptop for years. You're only just now seen it?"

"I've found a USB. Next Saturday, I'll bring it over and see what's on it. Don't forget tomorrow night at *L'Opera Mozart*."

"How can I? It's the only thing you've been talking about for the past month!"

***

Sunday morning, Louise and I hung the three paintings. I drilled the holes, inserted Rawlplugs and placed in wall hooks. I screwed in wire around the wooden border of the paintings and with Louise's eye correcting my hanging skills, I balanced the three paintings on the one wall.

We then covered them with white bed sheets of mine, courtesy of Remy, from the first time I'd had 'business dealings' with him. Sometime in the afternoon, Louise had completed her canapé preparations and I'd finished stacking the champagne bottles in the fridge.

Claude came down from his apartment and dramatically stopped in front of the three white cloths hanging over the paintings, "It looks like a room from a haunted house!"

Martin arrived, dressed for the event. He'd be helping us serve drinks and food again, and again for a cash incentive. Another cost I hadn't budgeted for!

I told him to sit guard over the paintings. "Do not lift the covers," I jokingly warned. "Louise remembers every crease, every carefully arranged fold." She kissed him and I left with her, both of us anxiously going home to dress.

As we passed Place Mozart, Louise asked, "What if no one comes?"

Chapter 12

It was the first Sunday in April—*Avril mi-printemps*—mid spring. My crazy idea was about to be put to the test. There was no way of avoiding it at this late stage. *Mozi-Art 1.0* was either going to be a success or an absolute failure.

Was I nervous? Did I have a feeling of dread in the pit of my stomach? Of course, I did. How do actors cope with an opening night?

I'd put on my well-cut blue suit, which Francine had bought me in Milan, a dark navy tie, polished patent leather shoes and, feeling particularly 'arty', my fedora, tilted rakishly over my right eye. On the outside, I certainly looked the part of an entrepreneur; however, on the inside, I felt a charlatan through and through.

I waited by the front door of my apartment for Louise to complete her final touches of make-up. I was itching to leave, and she sensed it, as she appeared from her bathroom. To ease my concern, she tried to wolf-whistle; however, being very nervous herself, she couldn't gather up enough spittle, nor lip formation to make a sound other than, "Wooh-wooh!"

We laughed at our childish excitement all the way down in the elevator. Once at *L'Opera Mozart,* I positioned myself by the front door, anxiously waiting to greet everyone, like I had been positioned at that society art event. *Learn from the experts, Dougay*, I heard my mother say.

Claude paced the cafe, likewise on edge, fearing the worse. That did not cheer me up. "It's my money, Claude," I consoled. That cheered him up.

That young, fit, bright-toothed couple arrived first, as they had at Madame St Romaine's art auction. He again presented beyond handsome and she as the ultimate male fantasy. He nodded warmly and she kissed me on both cheeks, as if I was known to them! They searched the café for a press photographer. Was that their *raison d'etre*? They were disappointed to find that I'd not invited any. I hadn't, because I don't need a public documentation of my failures!

I needn't have tried ignoring our local media, for Mimi Benoit, ace reporter, sauntered in. "I'm looking for Monsieur Dougay Roberre."

"That's me."

"You?" She queried. "You were the Maître d' at the art auction!" She stepped back to get a more appreciative look. "I expected…an art entrepreneur; sorry, someone older, more distinguished." Before I could take offence or laugh, she added, "I'd like to give this evening a paragraph in…" The young couple caught her eye and she hurried away.

"*Bonsoir*, Monsieur Entrepreneur." It was Remy. Once again, he had on both arms Angelie and Eloise, and wore a smile wide enough to embrace the two of them. All four of us warmly greeted each other, and I did not raise my suspicions.

Others now began to arrive. I was pleasantly surprised that many of them were strangers. Louise's dinners had brought in some, though this exhibition was bringing in many more. Locals I knew had decided to attend, along with faces I recognised from Madame St Romain's event four weeks earlier.

She'd said she'd lend her support for tonight's exhibition, and she had, spreading the word through her circle of friends and acquaintances, for which I was grateful.

I was now only managing to utter a welcome, before someone else walked in, shaking my hand, kissing my cheek, and wishing me *bonne chance*. I could get used to this. However, at the back of my mind, I knew if the night was a failure, I'd soon become the Riviera's most invisible man.

When Antoinette St Romain appeared out of the evening light, it was as if local artistic royalty had arrived on the café's doorstep. She stayed there, allowing everyone to see her presence, maintaining her position just inside the front door.

"Ah, Dougay, may this evening be all we hope it will be. It is wonderful to see you have re-established the nineteenth century vision of the café society in exhibiting artworks in local establishments. Congratulations, may the evening be a resounding success." She was unconcerned that people were lining up on the footpath behind her, wishing to get inside.

Martin was serving the champagne. I indicated he come over. He offered Madame St Romaine a flute of bubbly. She took one and stayed put.

Claude was carrying a tray of canapés. I called him over. He offered Madame St Romaine a rolled something in pastry. She took one and moved no further.

Louise was nervously watching, taking particular notice if Madame liked the canapé, she'd spent all afternoon creating. Seeing the logjam behind her, Louise indicated to me that I should usher in the grand dame and unclog the doorway. I gently placed my hand on Madame's back, easing her forward.

The stately woman entered, chewing and swallowing the contents of her hands, making a face of approval. Louise smiled once more.

Inside, towards the back room, the noise level was rising—a sure sign that people were enjoying themselves. I only hoped they'd still be enjoying themselves after the paintings had been revealed.

The three artists, my 'stars' of the evening, arrived as one, surprisingly linked in each other's arms, a triumvirate of mutual support. They'd momentarily buried any artistic differences, and had decided to make an 'entrance', to give their evening a theatrical kick.

Gabrielle Surmount, of course, was in the centre as if she was the Queen of Sheba, and the other two were mere Shebettes. She yelled, "We're here!" Heads turned and people applauded.

Gabrielle ran her hand down my crotch. I jumped! I introduced her to Remy.

"Wow!" She uttered. "You're the famous fighter, whose name I can't remember. Later in the evening, would you like to lay a knockout blow on me?" She held out her fists and laughed uproarishly.

Remy looked askance at me, his wide eyes asking, *who is this woman?*

I made no comment, because Francine stepped beside me. "Did that woman just run her hand down...?"

"Yes, I apologise for the brashness of Nice's artistic community."

"There is quite a deal of familiarity between artist and entrepreneur!" Francine laughed, then whispered, "I thought only I was allowed to do that." Before she could add anything further, her head turned. "Dougay, you remember Maurice, our mayor, don't you?"

I said, "Hello," though like last time, his eyes were elsewhere, checking out the room for potential swinging voters. I could have kissed Francine, danced a tango with her, tossed her to the floor, had my way with her, and he'd never have noticed. I thought I might try that later in the night—after a few champagnes had slid under my belt.

Francine held my hand a little too long. I got the impression she was feeling the same way about me.

All my friends came. For such a disparate bunch, they are very loyal. M'sieur and Madame Pom were dressed in their finest. As I reached for two glasses from Martin's tray, handing them over, M'sieur Pom asked, "Is that the mayor over there?" He knew full well it was. "And he's brought his fiancé!"

"I brought her," I corrected. Then fearing I may have stated too much implied information, I retreated. "She's actually my solicitor."

"You have a solicitor?" He asked, impressed.

Madame Legrande arrived with her two sons. As before, Raphael was with the impressive Doctor Armand and Pierre had that gorgeous nameless redhead on his arm. Luigi entered, once again escorting the blonde. I hoped for Luigi's sake, Pierre didn't deduct from his wage the blonde's fee for the evening.

When Pierre wasn't looking, I asked the redhead, "What's your name?"

"Pierre said you'd ask. That's the one thing I'm not allowed to tell you." She walked off laughing to join him.

My Czech contingency arrived, smuggling in frozen slivovitz in milk bottles. Milovic put on a pair of thick gloves and began rubbing the bottles. "Helps defrost them," he said, in answer to my quizzical look.

Ulna and her sister came close to me. Ulna made a point of saying out loud, so Milovic could hear, "In Czech Republic, we have an ancient custom. When welcoming a man, we women always kiss him three times!"

She did so, and so did Ljuba. Thankfully, her husband, Pasha, merely shook my hand.

Louise, ever the levelheaded organised one, came to me and said, "Stop enjoying yourself! It's time. Welcome everyone then introduce the paintings. Don't forget to do it in the order we agreed upon."

I squeezed past the guests and stepped nervously to the back wall where the paintings were hanging. Claude tapped a wine glass with a fork and I cleared my throat.

"Dear friends, I welcome you all. Thank you for coming. We have here tonight three excellent paintings to unveil for you. Keep in mind that the theme of *Mozi-Art 1.0* is Mozart represented in a humorous or satiric way. I believe our three artists here tonight have certainly captured that."

Most people were looking very strangely at me. Remy called out. "Hey mate! Not everyone here understands English!"

My nervousness had forced me onto my natural tongue, and I hadn't even realised it! They all laughed. I apologised and repeated my welcome in French. Inadvertently, I'd managed to break the tension in the room. Well, the tension running between Claude, Louise and me.

"Ladies and Gentleman, may I introduce the artist of our first painting—Monsieur Noel Fucheon." I pointed to the dapper, grey bearded gentleman in amongst the crowd. Everyone applauded warmly. Noel raised his glass and bowed his head, a gentleman through and through.

"His painting is entitled: *A Little Night Muzak.*"

Louise carefully removed the white bed sheet, unveiling the painting. There was a moment of silence, then a growing murmur, followed by a gasp of appreciation, capped off with a burst of applause.

Mozart was represented as an adult, seated at his keyboard, looking directly at the viewer, a long nightcap on his head. On the piano, there was a burning candle illuminating his music. Applause came again as people realised the composer had six fingers on his right hand and his eyes were decidedly crossed, making him look not like a genius, but rather the village idiot!

"Six fingers!" Someone shouted, immediately understanding the image. "No wonder he could play so well!"

People laughed! I didn't hurry things. I let them all enjoy the moment. After all, there were only three paintings, so I made an on-the-spot decision to adopt Jules' philosophy of stringing out the business at hand.

"Please, come forward to inspect more closely if you wish. People in front, can you move back to let the others through, please?"

After everyone had spent time in front of Noel's painting, I introduced Gabrielle Surmount, though I'm sure everyone knew her, or had heard of her and her 'artistic' reputation. She did a short wild dance, flinging her arms in the air. I think she may have forgotten that she held a glass of bubbly, for the contents were flung high in the air. Only Gabrielle Surmount could have managed to baptise the event with holy alcohol.

"Painting number two is titled: *Rondo a la Jerka.*"

Again Louise unveiled the painting. There was a moment of silent expectation, then a huge gasp of shock. Louise and I knew there would be. We exchanged conspiratorial glances, our eyes saying to each other, *I told you so!*

I stood well back from the painting and let everyone take it in. The applause came, accompanied by laughter and some sharp wolf whistling.

Gabrielle's painting was of Mozart as a child prodigy, sitting at the keyboard, banging on the keys, though not with his fingers. They were wrapped around his huge penis, which was slamming against the black and white ivories! It took quite a while for people to notice the small joint of marijuana in his mouth.

At this point, I didn't have to do much to elongate the proceedings—pardon the pun—as people's conversations generated a noisy vibrancy. Some of them forgot their sense of decorum, as they jostled to get a closer look, putting on reading glasses.

One rogue shouted, "Gabrielle! Who have you based that on?"

"No one I know!" Antoinette St Romain shouted back. Everyone laughed with appreciated irony. I was now well and truly relaxed, smiling broadly, for such outspoken humour could only be coming from a crowd clearly enjoying themselves.

Gabrielle walked to my position to address the guests. She pushed me aside, holding her arms up, waiting for the hubbub to die a little.

"He is based on," she shouted, "our benefactor—Dougay Roberre!"

My mouth fell open. People cheered. Francine was the only one, apart from me in the room, who knew she was lying! And then I recalled Madame Legrande had once undressed me, the time I'd been badly bashed out Aix-en-Provence way. I caught her eye. She was laughing louder than anyone else in the room!

Before Gabrielle stepped away, she planted a kiss on my lips. I kept my teeth clenched. "Spoil sport!" She whispered, slapping my shoulder.

Remy started a chant, "Dougay! Dougay! Dougay!"

I waved my arms in the air, eventually getting back control in the room. I didn't know the arty-farty types could be so raucous. Foolishly, as way of explanation, I shouted, joyously, "*Je suis un rockstar*!"

I heard Jules's shout, "You wish!"

The chant began again. "Dougay! Dougay! Dougay!"

To regain decorum in the room, Claude tapped his wine glass with his fork so hard it shattered. Eventually, everyone calmed.

I cleared my throat. "Artist number three is—Lautrelle Martin." He received dignified applause, more worthy of the mature nature of this event.

"Lautrelle's painting is called: *Queen of the Knife!*"

Louise stepped to the remaining covered painting and took hold of the bed sheet, pausing, bringing her own sense of drama to the unveiling. She eased the sheet from the upper two corners then whipped it down and stepped aside.

The room did not at first respond enthusiastically. Like Louise and I, when we first saw it last Wednesday, we did not know what to initially make of it. We did know; however, that it would have to be the last of the paintings revealed.

Lautrelle's painting was a portrait of the child Mozart kneeling before Marie-Antoinette, asking for her hand in marriage. It was a faithful representation of the supposed true event, immaculately realised in a photographic realism of glorious colour.

The striking feature of the painting was that Marie-Antoinette's beautiful head was completely severed, lying on the floor at her feet, her eyes looking back up to where her head should have been on the end of her long and bloodied neck.

People gawped. "*Mon Dieu!*" Someone cried out, "That's Marie Antoinette, before she became Dauphine of France!"

A growing murmur rippled through the room. A voice began singing 'La Marseillaise'. It grew louder and stronger, the gathered voices uniting as one. By the time everyone was singing, "*Marchons! Marchons!*" I was a quivering mess of tingles and ice cold shivers.

Chapter 13

Around midnight, Louise, Claude, Martin and I sat in the empty café, neither of us wanting to leave. We were talking over the evening's events, commenting again and again on the euphoria which had gripped the room. We could not let, nor did we want to let, the moment go.

"The mayor was here," said a chuffed Claude. "What an honour!"

"Which one was he?" Louise asked.

"My solicitor is actually engaged to him," explained Claude. "The woman with jet black hair, rather tall, carries herself as if she may have been a model at one time." Even though he was aware of my feelings for Francine, Claude did not make for Louise the connection between Francine and me.

Claude needn't have bothered. Thinking about the description, Louise declared, "Oh, the woman who could not take her eyes off Dougay?"

"What?" I asked, surprised. "She is also my solicitor, as well, Louise. She drew up the artist's contracts. She was probably wondering how a loser like me could come up with such a winning idea."

I could tell Louise thought that a distinct possibility. We all simultaneously sipped our well-earned drink.

"I have met the mayor," I mused, "twice now, and both times he's ignored me. However, tonight as he was leaving, he couldn't let go of my hand."

Claude smiled, "You have arrived, Dougay. I know I'm being cynical, but I heard him ask his secretary who you were."

"Which one was he?" Louise asked. "The mayor's secretary?"

"The nervous looking man," Claude said. "Furtive, possessive eyes."

"Guy Germaine," I added, wondering how I'd so easily remembered his name after that one meeting at the art exhibition. "He's a pompous little egoist." Before they could ask how I knew that, I changed tack.

"Yes, Claude, Francine has introduced me to the mayor both times our paths have crossed. The mayor knows full well who I am."

"Maybe he wasn't listening," said Martin. "Politicians are notorious for claiming they do, though do they really?"

"Martin, you're a bit young to be so cynical, aren't you?" I asked.

"Age is no barrier to cynicism, particularly when it comes to politicians," said Louise, defending Martin.

"Yes," continued Claude, "politicians are only interested in those who can further their aspirations. Or those whom they think can benefit them in a photographic opportunity. Thank yourself lucky, Dougay, you aren't a baby and he wanted to kiss you."

"Yuk!" Louise laughed.

"Here's to a great success," said Claude, raising his near empty glass in toast. Louise, Martin and I joined him and all four of us declared, "To a great success!"

We knocked back our glasses. Claude added cheekily, "It was a wonderful idea of mine!"

***

I woke late in the morning, and feeling mentally exhausted, strolled into Place Mozart, sans coffee, sans breakfast. If I smoked, then this was the time I'd probably have a lonely, contemplative drag. Instead, I sat and exhaled deeply the fresh air in my garden of solitude.

A dog wandered over and cocked his leg. Before he could relieve himself, I moved to Madame Legrande's favourite bench. A minute later, M'sieur Pom walked over to me.

"This makes a change," I said. "I've never seen you here before."

"Yes, I had to ask my wife for directions." He laughed at his gag, easing down next to me, and carefully opened his newspaper, as if it contained precious state secrets.

He read out loud, *Mini Exhibit—Maxi Sensation! By arts reporter Mimi Benoit.* He made an issue of clearing his throat before going on.

In an ordinary cafe, in an ordinary street, in an ordinary suburb of Nice, an extraordinary exhibition awaits. Mozi-Art 1.0 is a sensation waiting to unfold before your eyes. Three satiric paintings hang on a wall, waiting to take your breath away.

One possesses the cheekiness of subtle artist, Noel Fucheon; a second displays the raw confrontational sexuality of that genius we've come to both admire and be confronted by, Gabrielle Surmount; and a third, by artist Lautrelle Martin, dares to stir nationalistic fervour with its heart wrenching, resounding echoes of the events leading up to our Revolution.

For a red-blooded French man and woman, it is the most relevant portrait of Marie-Antoinette ever realised!

Take a plane, take a train, take a bus, or simply walk there, but get there in the next four weeks or you'll miss out on seeing the most inspiring and satiric mini-exhibition you'll ever experience. Where? L'Opera Mozart Cafe, Nice, Cote d'Azur.

I sat, overwhelmed by the review. M'sieur Pom stayed sitting with me. Two minutes later, I nudged him in the side. "Read it again."

***

That evening Claude informed me, "We had more people through today, and remember it's only Monday, than we've ever totalled for the first three days of our best week."

"Yes," I commented, my hands in sudsy dishwater, "I can tell. There's a lot more washing up to be done."

"They're coming to look at the paintings and staying to buy coffee and cake. As I said last night, it was a wonderful idea of mine."

I didn't bite. I was pleased Claude was happy with how things were turning out, though I couldn't let the moment pass

163

entirely. "First his music, then Louise's cooking, now the portraits. You have to admit I get some crazy left field ideas, which sometimes pay off."

Claude mockingly sneered at me. "I can't stay and debate the facts with you, Monsieur Entrepreneur. I have to order extra croissants for tomorrow."

Late Tuesday morning, the cafe's phone rang. My hands were in suds again, washing up the coffee cups and saucers and cake-stained plates, which kept coming my way. Claude was enjoying dropping them into the sink and wandering off singing.

As the phone continued to ring, I called out, "Get that would you, Claude, please. I have washerwoman's hands."

"You're such a sexist pig, Dougay," he said, jokingly. I couldn't believe Claude had now been joyously happy for two whole days!

"It's for you!" He said, surprised. I wiped my hands and took the receiver from him.

I listened and finally said, "Okay, see you then."

I handed the receiver back to him.

"Well?" He asked.

"Local newspaper—ace reporter Mimi Benoit, wants a personal interview with me concerning my exhibition; 2pm this afternoon."

Claude ignored me big noting myself. Rubbing his hands with glee, he walked off singing that show tune, *If I were a Rich Man*!

***

On Wednesday morning, I sat with Madame Legrande in Place Mozart. I had my head back looking at the sky, wishing summer was here, when she nudged me in the ribs. I looked down to see M'sieur Pom coming into the garden, carrying his morning newspaper.

He held it open, proudly, in front of his chest as he came to us. There was a photo of me standing next to the painting of the headless Marie-Antoinette. Mozart had been cropped from the shot. "I know someone famous!" M'sieur Pom kidded.

Madame Legrande, after studying it for what seemed an eternity, said nothing, she merely squeezed my arm and wouldn't let go.

M'sieur Pom read out the interview I'd given. It was a near exact transcription of what I'd said; not embarrassing at all. Mimi Benoit was rising in my estimation.

"Madame, Dougay," began M'sieur Pom, "not only the photograph and interview, I came across this as well. It might be of interest, seeing that we visited only a little while ago." We both looked at him, not knowing to what he was eluding.

"A Nice councillor, Madame Janvre, who represents the area over towards Villefranche-sur-Mer, has asked a question at last night's city council meeting." He read from the paper.

Is there any truth in the rumour that some parklands are being considered for rezoning? "Of course, the mayor denied such claims. She went on." *In particular, some 'underutilised areas' inside, or attached to Parc de L'Eco-Vallee?* "Interesting, is it not, seeing as how we were only up there recently?"

We sat a while longer, considering that. When M'sieur Pom returned inside, I said to Madame Legrande, "Madame, when we were up at that park, I nodded off when you were speaking of that friend of yours, who you all went to school with. I showed you her daughter's photo, remember?"

"I remember. What are you up to now, Dougay?"

"Madame, trust me, have I ever let you down?"

"No, apart from my two boys, you are the only man who can claim that."

I put on my serious voice. "Can you explain the circumstances again, please?"

She looked at me, still with a trace of suspicion in her eyes. "Moni Flourent, rather, Moni Goumas, had a very rude awakening. Her husband ran off with a younger woman. That's hardly new. But before he did, he moved all her wealth, which she'd inherited from her parents, into new accounts he'd set up. He left her penniless."

"And the daughter? Would she be penniless?"

"No, she has her job. Though up until the time her father took flight, she'd always had everything she could possibly ask for."

"That would be hard to get over. I wonder how they're coping."

"The daughter is fine. She has a job, rents a simple but attractive apartment, though she probably gives her mother something, top up her wage as a child's nurse. The mother would be the one at the end of every month needing money."

*****

The crowds kept building. M'sieur Pom said that *Mozi-Art 1.0* was spoken in passing on Parisian television and mentioned in both *Paris-Match* and *Le Monde*.

Thursday morning, I was again at the kitchen sink of *L'Opera Mozart*. Lately, that sink was becoming my home away from home!

"Claude," I said, as he passed to wipe down the outside tables after the local breakfast crowd had drifted off. "I was not aware that famous entrepreneurs still had to do the washing up!" He scoffed and continued outside.

I wiped my dishwasher's hands as I turned from the sink. Jules St Croix stood before me on the other side of the counter.

"What are you doing here?" I asked, surprised.

"Any chance of a coffee?" He asked, licking his dry lips.

I made two and we carried them outside past the people waiting to see the paintings, to the table next to Old Hector, who studied Jules. We sipped our hot coffee. Old Hector leant in and in a soft voice enquired, "Pardon, Monsieur, are you Jules St Croix?"

Jules was suddenly wary. He quickly studied the old man and glanced around fearing he may be watched, or worse, set upon.

"This is Hector," I explained, trying to ease Jules' noticeable concern. "He's our most regular customer."

"Yes, Hector Laurent," the old man said. "My younger brother is Louis. I believe you may have gone to school with him."

Jules thought for a moment. "Yes! Louis Laurent! A snappy halfback! He could score a try from anywhere on the field. How is he doing?"

"He's now onto his fourth wife. He cannot keep his doodle in his trousers."

"Ah," said Jules. "Sadly, I cannot find a woman to pull mine out!"

We all laughed, though I hoped it wasn't true, as I knew nothing of Jules' personal life. They chatted further. I only half listened, because they spoke of acquaintances of whom I had no inkling.

Old Hector bid us farewell, pleased with the catch up of reminiscences liberally coated with male laughter.

I turned to Jules. "What are you doing over this way?" I asked, bringing the conversation back into focus.

"Just passing."

"Jules, I do not believe that for one minute."

"Okay, I wish to ask you some questions. I want you to answer them truthfully."

"Have I ever lied to you?"

He ignored my question. "Paul Villan—how do you know him?"

I paused, considering. "Okay, I'll explain. The first time I came across him, I was not fully introduced. I had no idea who he was, only that his first name was Paul. I learned his full name the second time I came across him when I was working as the Maître d' at an art event held at *Le Grande Nice*."

Jules raised his eyebrows. He seemed to be impressed.

"The first time I met him? Francine Delange delivered Paul the money from a property sale. I was there as protection. I had a skirmish with two goons belonging to the Mascati twins, who not only wanted the property they also wanted back the money they'd paid for it."

"*Mon Dieu!*" He whispered. "The Mascati twins!" I do not know if he was impressed with my bravery or my stupidity.

"Wait!" I said, remembering fully. "After that, you drove Francine and me back from Milan!"

"Ah, that time. Yes, I may have driven you, though I never knew the reason."

"So, Francine does not give you the entire picture, as well?"

"It's safer that way—for her, for me, for you." He let that sink in; however, that may not have been the reason for his pause in the conversation, for he asked, "Any chance of a second cup of coffee?" I went off to replenish both our mugs.

When I returned, Jules went on. "Answer me some questions about the human condition."

"I'm not a philosopher, Jules."

He ignored me, blowing on top of his mug to cool it.

"What was Paul Villan doing up there, in that park, with that woman? Was it spiritual?"

"Spiritual? No!"

"Was it social?"

"Social?" I queried, not knowing where these questions could possibly be leading.

"Yes, social," reinforced Jules. "Was he introducing her to a wider range of friends?"

"No, of course not. You were there. There was no one else around."

"Was it a moment of sustenance?"

"Sustenance?"

"Yes. Did they share food and drink?"

"A picnic? No."

"Was it sexual?" I'll say one thing for Jules he is persistent with his line of questioning.

"No. You know it wasn't."

"So, finally, was it financial?" He asked, leaning into me across the table. I didn't answer. I had no idea if it was or it wasn't. "Yes, *mon ami*," admitted Jules, "that we do not know, do we? So, if we can't eliminate it, then perhaps it was financial."

We both thought about that. Then Jules asked, "Remember that photo you asked I send you? Do you know that woman, Madame Petain's friend?"

"At the time I didn't, but I do now."

"Ah, good, I knew there was a reason I came over here to chat with you. What's her name?"

"Avril Goumas."

"And in that building where she works, do you know what department employs her?"

"*Parcs, Jardins et Promenades.*"

"Thank you, my friend." He stood to leave.

"It can't be financial, Jules. She doesn't need the money, surely. She has a well-paid job. She's number two in the organisation." And then I had a thought.

"However, Avril's mother might need the money, because she doesn't have a well-paid job. She's a child's nurse. And before that, she'd been used to a life of not going without."

Jules smiled knowingly, as if I'd solved the riddle of the century.

"Jules, Paul Villan moves in questionable circles," I warned. "Keep your head down."

"Oh, I intend to. And to keep the rest of my body at a discreet distance."

***

On Friday and Saturday evenings, *L'Opera Mozart* once again offered Louise's special dinner menu. Both nights, the cafe was full, and everyone wanted to have their photograph taken with the paintings.

Noel Fucheon's painting gathered studied appreciation. Smiles, rather than belly laughs, emanated from those who stood in front of it.

Gabrielle's painting continued to attract a lot of lingering looks. One man, to the delight of his friends, claimed he was the model for it! One female stranger asked him for his phone number, causing friction with his wife, and a near punch-up between their respective husbands.

However, the painting which was creating the most interest was Lautrelle's. It seemed to be taking on a reverential aura amongst those who came to view it. Someone placed a lit candle on the floor beneath it. I soon got rid of that, as I didn't know what political intention was meant by its placement there. Raphael Legrande's warning, about remaining apolitical in business, rang in my ears.

The Local Minister for Tourism's Secretary rang the café asking for an appointment so he could visit and have his photograph taken with the paintings. I 'umed' and 'ahed' a little. The secretary said that he'd like me to be in the photo as well. *Me?* How could I refuse? Secretly, I was rather enjoying my fifteen minutes of fame.

On the Saturday afternoon, I headed to Remy's warehouse for our regular spar. I had the USB stick in my pocket, as I still had not purchased a laptop. I thumped on his metal roller door and he opened the single steel one. He looked terrible.

"Are you okay?" I asked.

"Exhausted. I don't think I'll be sparring today."

He ushered me in. I sat at his desk waiting for his explanation. "You're to blame," he said.

"Me?" I asked, incredulously.

"Yes, if it wasn't for you, I'd have never met that woman."

My immediate thought was that Angelie had got the better of him during one of their boxing lessons. He must have let his guard down, as Remy never came off second best to anyone.

"Sunday night, I left your *Mozi-Art* event, with that painter!"

"Gabrielle Surmount?" I asked, flabbergasted. "You picked up Gabrielle Surmount and took her home?"

"Yes. Gabi! Not to my home, here—to her home—her studio, actually." I couldn't say a word, for my eyes were wide and my tongue was tied. "What a woman! What a night! She rolled me on the floor between unfinished canvasses and drop cloths and tubes and jars of paints. I've still got a red and green ass!"

He turned and whipped down his pants. He wasn't joking! At that moment, I wished I was red-green colour blind!

"And you're still recovering from Sunday night? Apart from rooting amongst the colours of the rainbow, what did she do to you?"

"I've never been so comprehensively, you know. And it wasn't only Sunday night. I went back Monday night, Tuesday night, Wednesday night, Thursday night, and Friday night."

"And where are you going tonight?" I asked, cheekily.

"The hospital—recovery ward." He did not laugh. I did.

"Alright, alright, that's enough," he admonished me, as if I was a naughty child. As if *I* was a naughty child!

"So, you're serious, when you say we're not sparring?" I asked, needing clarification. Remy said that he needed medication.

"Yes, I must be getting old," he added meekly. "I've never missed a sparring session in my life."

I held up the USB. He opened his laptop and booted it up. I handed the stubby stick to him. As he stuck it into the side of the computer, I dragged around a chair and we sat side by side. He clicked and wiggled his mouse.

There was only one file on it. It read: 'Naughty Nora Charles'.

Chapter 14

Remy clicked on the file. It was a video. I hoped it had a good story. It didn't. However, it was riveting all the same.

A computer generated graphic flashed on the laptop's screen reading: *Naughty Nora Charles*. It cut to a second graphic: *Her Adventures in Paradise*. A third followed: *Round One*.

Two women were sparring. I'm not a fan of women fighting. However, these women, for protection, were wearing the correct gloves. That was all they were wearing. Angelie Faivre and Belinda Swann were totally naked. They'd been boxing for a while, as both were wet with perspiration.

As a demonstration of boxing technique, I'd say that Remy had taught Angelie pretty well. As an example of soft porn, I'd say both women needed no further instruction. They'd mastered the genre.

I hit the space bar and froze the fight. Remy did not complain. Was he watching this? I looked sideways. His body position and facial expression had not changed from when the first title flashed up. I guess Gabi's impact this past week was hard to shake off.

Without commenting, Remy tapped the space bar and the two women continued, throwing punches, ducking and weaving. As I said, I don't like watching women fight, though this was only sparring, and as no one was getting hurt, I accepted that it was an advanced work out session.

Both women, I admit, were two exceptional examples of the female form, and therefore, I was not watching for the violence, rather for the appreciation of the balletic merits on display. At times, I do like to delude myself.

Not many blows landed and those that did were only half-heartedly delivered. Some were followed by suppressed apologies and giggles.

When Round One was over, they hugged each other and kissed! Holy hell! I confess I instinctively turned my face away, feeling they needed some privacy. I was embarrassed for them. Or was that for me? I wasn't thinking too straight. However, their tongues were straight, extending from their mouths, flicking each other, as if in a duel at dawn.

Remy continued to remain silent. Perhaps, he'd never fully realised until now, what I'd try to explain to him about Angelie and her preference for women.

The video cut to a shower scene. I groaned out loud and hit the space bar. "Look at that!" I said. "A cream shower with a maroon trim. Where would that be, Remy?" I asked pointedly, knowing full well where it was.

He didn't answer. I went on. "That's the basement in the building where your mate, Serge, works as caretaker!"

Still Remy said nothing.

"Do you know anything about this?" I looked at him, waiting for an answer. "Oh hell!" I exclaimed. "You're the one holding the camera! That's why you're not as interested in watching this video as I am. You've seen this movie before! How does it end? Does the heroine get the girl? Do they ride off into the sunset together?"

I waited for his reply. He took his time. "Angelie and Belinda are old friends."

"No, they're not," I immediately countered.

"They're lovers!" He insisted.

"Okay, okay, I see they're lovers; however, they're not old friends. When those two walked into that basement, was Belinda dressed as a man? In a cream grey vested trouser suit?"

"How do you know that?" He asked, surprised.

I wasn't about to tell him. Instead, I said, "They're not old friends. They met only four weeks ago at a Society Art Event. I was there. I was Maître d' for the night. Eloise saw Belinda Swann turn up incognito and phoned Angelie, who drove down from Eze, dressed like a million bucks.

"She turned every head in the restaurant; however, she was only interested in turning the head of Belinda Swann! I'd say Angelie, after propositioning Belinda with some perverse come-on, drove her back up to Eze, where she's satisfied every perversion that Belinda ever craved. Then she's suggested the next day they go to Serge's basement and make a movie for a keepsake.

"When Angelie phoned you, asking you to film it, did she also ask you to make the studio booking with Serge?"

Remy didn't answer. He didn't have to. His silence was confirmation enough.

"Whatever sexual delight Angelie offered Belinda, it was special, for it kept Belinda hidden up there on Angelie's farm, away from Belinda's lesbian coterie back here in Nice, for three days. It was three days, because I know on the fourth day, Belinda Swann was driven to the airport, on the supportive arm of her dead husband's old school pal, Beau Andrews. They flew out of Nice together."

I hit the space bar and the two women sank to the floor of the shower, water cascading over them, as they luridly kissed for Remy's camera.

"Remy, how'd you manage to keep the camera still?" I asked, sarcastically, making no apology for the fact that my own blood pressure was rising.

"I'm a professional," he said, undercutting my previous rave. We both snorted a suppressed laugh, easing the tension between us.

Another graphic flashed up: *Round Two*.

It contained more of the same—punches thrown and missed and dodged and weaved and breasts bouncing and butts tightly vibrating, all liberally coated in perspiration. And of course, there followed another shower scene, in which they were far more relaxed in each other's arms than previously.

Belinda Swann clearly enjoyed whatever she turned her mind to, because she was groaning, her body trembling. I sarcastically commented, "What a professional! She never once looks at the camera." Belinda let out a cry of ecstasy. "She may be an actress, but she's not acting now!"

"You are correct," Remy finally conceded. "This was made by Angelie for Belinda to take back to the States, to remember her until the next time she was in Cannes." He hit the space bar. "That's it. That's all I filmed."

I looked at the bottom of the screen. "It's not over, Remy. Look!" I pointed to the time line. "There's still a third to go." I hit the space bar. A graphic appeared: *Round Three*.

Remy slammed his hand onto the space bar, freezing the title. "I didn't film a round three. I only did two evenings—Monday and Tuesday, a couple of weeks back." He looked at me as if he'd never seen me before. "How did you get this video?"

I let the question hang. "You weren't asked to film the third round. Why? Because you'd have objected and put a stop to it. You'd have ruined Angelie's and Eloise's plan."

"What plan? You sound like a conspiracy theorist."

"Revenge." I had no idea of the detail, which was coming in round three, though I sure knew the outcome. I'd picked it up from the pavement outside my apartment block.

I hit the space bar. Round three was not set in Serge's basement. This room was much darker. A naked Belinda Swann, her arms stretched and tied above her head, was moving seductively for the camera. She was teasing, her tongue poking out of tempting, pouting lips. She had no idea what was coming her way, as she leant against something that couldn't remain still.

"That's my large boxing bag!" Remy exclaimed. "That's the one I took up to Angelie's farm. I hung it in her barn." Then he realised, "That's the barn where I taught Angelie to fight!"

The background sure looked like a barn, though it was hard to tell, because the writhing, sensually excited Belinda Swann in the foreground dominated the proceedings. The back of a naked woman came into the frame. There was something on her head. I hit the space bar, freezing the image.

"What's that on that woman's head? It's still Angelie, isn't it?"

"Yes. That's the way I taught her to hold her fists," admitted Remy, admiring his coaching skills.

"What is it?" I peered closer into the screen. "Is that a mask?"

"A superhero mask," qualified Remy, now as interested as I had been at the outset.

"What's Belinda Swann's famous sci-fi character called?" I asked, clicking my fingers, as if somehow the answer was there on its tips.

"*Mademoiselle America!*"

"Is that who that mask represents? Is Belinda Swann about to be hit by her own fictional character?" We studied the frozen screen, Remy nodding, agreeing. "What were those films she made with that dead husband of hers?" I asked.

"*Gothila*," he said. "The other one was *Gothila's Revenge*."

"This *Mademoiselle America*, is that the character she played in them?"

"I think so, yes!"

I hit the space bar. Belinda began smiling, enjoying the moment. Unbeknownst to her, the soft porn video was about to get a lot harder. She teased, "Come on, *Mademoiselle America*, hit me. I've been naughty!"

Masked Angelie did, a lot harder than Belinda imagined or expected. I winced as the first blow struck.

Remy let out a strangled, "*Merde!*"

The blow knocked the wind out of Belinda Swann. Again, she wasn't acting. She dangled against the large boxing bag, gasping for air.

Angelie stepped back, studying her. As Belinda began to gather breath and raise her head, Angelie stepped in and sent a low upper cut into her torso, immediately below the rib cage.

"You've taught her well, Remy," I said, with no sense of congratulations in my voice.

Belinda, held against the bag, was forced back by the momentum of the impact, the bag returning her for a third and fourth savage blow. Angelie, stepping away again, prolonged the tortuous beating.

Belinda looked to Angelie. In her eyes, one could read she knew the sexual games Angelie and her had been playing for the past three days, were now over. She uttered, painfully, "Do your fucking best, bitch!"

Angelie did. She pummelled her. After thirty seconds, the flurry of blows began to seriously weaken Belinda's resolve and stamina.

I heard Eloise say from behind the camera, "Hit her again in the ribs."

Belinda looked to the side of Angelie, to the voice behind the camera.

"Recognise her?" A heavy breathing Angelie asked.

Belinda uttered a breathless, "No."

"Eloise is one of your victims. You scratched her so deeply you've probably still got her DNA under your finger nails."

"Give her one for the death of Danielle Hubert. Hit her in the kidneys," Eloise ordered. "Hurt the bitch!"

Angelie did, over and over. It was savage and cruel and vindictive and revengeful. Belinda Swann hung there on Remy's large boxing bag, her head flopped to one side, like a piece of beef, waiting to be sliced into various expensive cuts.

As a parting gesture, Angelie hit her a final time on the cheek. Belinda's head spun, saliva flying from her mouth.

A final graphic came up over a close up of Belinda's smashed face. It read: *Think twice before returning to Nice.* I hit the space bar. Our Saturday matinee at the movies was over.

"I had nothing to do with that last round," said Remy, sitting back in his chair, stunned by the viciousness of his pupil.

"You've been had, Remy. Months ago, Angelie began planning her revenge on Belinda Swann, for what she'd done to her lover, Eloise. That's how long ago she asked you to teach her to box. Only for fitness purposes, she'd said. Remember?"

We sat in silence for a while. "I'm sorry I took you up to her farm with me."

"I drove. You could never have walked there." He stretched out his legs and sighed. "Every decision I've ever made has been made by me."

I said nothing. I left his desk and searched the warehouse. In Remy's toolbox, I found a hammer and a cloth. I wrapped the USB into the cloth and placed it onto the concrete floor.

"What are you doing?" Remy asked.

I held up the hammer. "What does it look like?"

"You don't wish to view it a second time?"

I snorted at Remy's black humour. I lifted the hammer and smashed the smithereens out of the USB, tipping the shattered pieces into Remy's waste paper basket.

"We could have made a fortune out of that, on the internet," Remy said, staring at his bin. At times, he has such a perfectly dry delivery, I never know if he is serious or not.

"That's why I destroyed it. Protection for all involved; including you and me." I returned the hammer and closed the toolbox. I came back to him, put my hand on his shoulder and quietly asked, "Want to go over to *Vlatava-Elbe* and knock back some slivovitz?"

"At this hour? It's only afternoon."

"I have a taste in my mouth I need to get rid of."

"I've the same taste."

"Come on, let's go."

Chapter 15

I was sitting in Place Mozart, head back, looking skyward, and once again thinking of the promise summer would bring. I thought about calling Mary-Anne tonight to see if she had any idea when she'd be returning from New York. I recalled being on the beach at Villefranche-sur-Mer with Francine, and being on that nameless beach over near the Italian border with Mary-Anne.

I'd love to repeat both experiences this summer, though I would be happy with only the one. *Which one?* was the question I often posed myself, wasting time in Place Mozart.

I had come to believe that Francine and Mary-Anne were really two sides of the same coin, both spinning in the air, most of the time out of reach, and I knew when I did get to hold the coin, it would only be held for a moment. I shouldn't really complain, I suppose, because simply getting my fingers on the coin was a most wonderful experience.

I was woken from my reverie by M'sieur Pom plonking himself beside me on the park bench.

"That's where Madame Legrande usually sits," I told him. "She's much prettier than you."

"And you," he reminded me.

"Touché."

"Look." He showed me the front page of the morning newspaper. I took it from him and studied it. There was a photograph of developer Paul Villan with Avril Goumas.

"What does the caption say, M'sieur Pom?"

He read: 'Property Developer Paul Villan and Assistant Parks Manager Avril Goumas together at Parc de L'Eco-Vallee'. He ran his finger under the larger printed word: *Why?*

"The article goes on to say that there are expected to be more questions asked by Madame Janvre, city councillor, at the next meeting. Further over, there's an editorial, which reinforces everyone's love of that park, and the importance of maintaining green spaces. It also hints at greed—the selling of public spaces to developers, who then erect ugly concrete towers."

He put down the paper. "Someone at the newspaper is starting to get a sniff of something. Corruption? Speculation always allows rumour and innuendo to blossom." He tapped his finger on the newspaper. "This photograph is hardly posed for. Look at it." He passed it to me again. "It's taken from behind a palm tree."

Yes, it had been, and it was one of the photographs I'd asked Jules to take. I wondered how far he and Paul Villan went back, and what the property developer had done to the P.I. to make him wait so long for a subtle revenge.

Or was this photograph placed to thwart someone not in the frame? Like Felicity Deschamps for not paying Jules' outstanding account?

If so, how did Jules know the connection between her and Paul Villan? *Yes*, I remembered. I'd told him about seeing them outside that bar, the night I escorted Sue-Lin home. It surely wasn't that mention of a brief encounter, was it? Jules must have known of a stronger connection between the two, for like all places, Nice's social threads run deep and long.

Maybe it wasn't about Felicity at all, I finally speculated. *Maybe Jules is just a true 'greenie' at heart.*

Only time would tell how it was going to play out, though I didn't think embarrassing Felicity Deschamps would get her to hand over Jules' money.

"I find this murky, wheeling and dealing world quite fascinating," admitted M'sieur Pom. "Who's up who and why; enthralling stuff."

"One day you should write it all down and compile a book. It could be an extensive spider's web of Riviera intrigue."

He didn't say 'no' to the idea, merely looking at me as if he was considering the possibility for the first time. "*Un Nice Noir?*" He contemplated. "You remember ten or twelve years back, Paul Villan…"

"I've only been in France for a year."

"Of course. Well, ten or twelve years ago, if memory serves me correctly, Paul Villan returned from a holiday in England, or the United States, I can't remember exactly where, to find the rotting corpse of his mother or aunt, some close female relative, in some building she'd owned."

"Natural causes?"

"Yes, there was no foul play. Names and odd events stick with me, though not always the precise details."

"Is this the same Paul Villan?"

"Oh, yes. Property and Paul go hand in hand."

I moved the conversation along. "Any more updates on the bed hoping exploits of the ex-deputy mayor and his wife?"

"They'll never get back together. She's already castrated him, courtesy of that front page expose last year."

"Why would she do that?" I pondered out loud.

"It's obvious—to get back at her cheating husband."

I wanted M'sieur Pom to do a little thinking for me, so I prompted him. "What if that's 'not' the reason?" I suggested. "Well, it obviously was, but let's say since then things have changed. Let's say some things aren't as obvious as they seem." I still had that image of her husband grabbing her playfully on her ass!

"What? A diversion?" M'sieur Pom was now thinking cunningly, in tune with me. "Send the world in a different direction?" He pondered.

I sat up a little straighter. "Have you ever been conned by those fast-moving shells, with the pea underneath one of them? Or wondered how they cut a woman in half?"

"Do you mean one hand dances before your eyes, while the other steals from your pocket?"

"Maybe."

"No. Pierre Deschamps' ambition was to be mayor," said M'sieur Pom, returning to what he knew. "He blew that chance when he was photographed in bed with that blonde."

"What if his ambition, or rather Felicity's ambition, isn't only for him to be mayor for the political and social kudos attached to it, but to hold the position for what it gives him and by association, her."

I had his full attention now.

"Access," I explained. "Access to everything in Nice. Papers, town records, council plans, influence, and the ability to re-zone areas. Information and permission are mightily powerful things to have under one's control. Under the responsibility of some people, it can result in them filling their wallet. Remember, you once said to me, why steal ten euro in daylight when you can steal ten thousand from behind a smoke screen?"

"I was not aware my words made such an impression on you, Dougay. I am pleased my philosophies have lingered inside your head."

"How far away is the Monaco border?" I prodded him. "That tax haven is just over there." I added, pointing off to the east.

"So, Dougay, you're implying that as long as Pierre Deschamps was the loyal deputy mayor, agreeing to everything Maurice St Romain said and did, he'd always be held back in the shadow of his running mate and the constraints of his political party?"

"And this public exposure allows us to be blindsided to their newly formed desires. I think you're right, and you've always said that one day he'll make a run for the top job. That is once he has spent enough time in the political wilderness. You know, penance in the public eye. When Deschamps makes his move, the current mayor will need to watch his back."

"I don't think Deschamps is that cunning."

"Ever seen or read Shakespeare's *MacBeth*?"

"Felicity Deschamps as Lady MacBeth?" M'sieur Pom seriously considered the idea.

"Let's suppose the public scandal really began as an act of revenge," I said. "Let's say Felicity paid for the blonde and for the whole set up." Of course, I already knew Felicity had paid Jules and me to burst in and take the photos, though I was not going to tell M'sieur Pom that particular detail.

"And after the exposé," M'sieur Pom continued on from my idea, "she's had another thought, a deeper thought—a more financially beneficial thought."

"Yes, a thought which means access to real money."

He nodded, contemplating, "Perhaps she's forgiven him and replaced her feelings of infidelity with greed; her desire for revenge being well and truly supplanted."

"Could be," I mused. "M'sieur Pom, you're more devious than she is."

"Speculation, Dougay, mere speculation." We both nodded. "It's just a feeling I have, but there's always been a suspect look in Felicity Deschamps' eyes."

"M'sieur Pom, the police can't arrest someone for having a certain look in their eyes."

***

The next morning, M'sieur Pom showed me the newspaper. "Paul Villan has denied everything. He claims it was a rendezvous, as simple as that. Lovers out for a stroll. When pushed for more detail regarding this affair, he admitted: 'It's early days. We only recently met at an art auction'. It's the one you were at Dougay, *The Society for the Advancement of Artistic Expression, Endeavour and Realisation on the Cote d'Azur*. The woman has made no comment."

"I wonder why the media have only mentioned her name in a photo's caption and not hounded her to make a statement."

"Do not wonder too long, Dougay. They'll be doing that as we speak."

Paul Villan did not meet Avril Goumas at that society art event. She was never there. I should know, I was on the door, checking every name. I recalled Paul Villan had arrived with Eloise Pittard.

He'd left with Felicity Deschamps and later met up with her husband in that bar of that posh hotel down by the water. That overlapping conversation now made sense. That was when they'd put their heads together and decided to make a play for the rezoning of the park, and Jules' published photograph had brought the matter to light and hopefully stifled their long-term plans.

The newspaper had reprinted the photograph in half size, though Avril's face was still clearly recognisable. I wondered what her friends, who she had lunch with, were making of this.

"Why repeat the photograph, M'sieur Pom?"

"They will say: 'In the name of public interest'. Though more in the name of selling papers, pedalling innuendo, and ruining reputations."

We fell to silence. A car came up from the car park and we watched it drive away without comment. Almost as an afterthought," I muttered, "I know where that woman works."

"The one driving that car which just left?"

"No, Avril Goumas."

"Dougay, I wonder if she's okay. If you know her, you should ring to see how she's getting on. I'd like to know. No one likes their photo on the front page unless they crave publicity. She could well be an innocent in all of this."

He turned to me, and placing his hand on my knee, he softly reinforced, "I'd be interested in knowing."

"To be honest, so would I. Though what should I say? No, I can't call, as my voice may be recognised." He looked at me puzzled. I didn't explain. Searching, I found the number for the city administration centre and dialled it. I handed M'sieur Pom my phone.

"*Bonjour*, Madame," he said, politely. "May I speak to Avril Goumas, please? She's attached to Parks and Gardens."

He listened for a moment. "*Merci*, Madame." He ended the call, handing me back my mobile. "She's not in her office. She's ill. Ah well, we tried."

"I think there may be another way to find out for you. Come on."

We crossed to Madame Legrande's apartment. She opened her door and was genuinely surprised to see both of us standing there.

"Madame," I began, "could you do a favour for us, please?"

Madame Legrande invited us in. I explained to her that I'd like her to make a phone call. She did, willingly.

"Moni, Moni Goumas? Yes, yes, it's me. That's wonderful. Yes, yes, you also. Moni, what a shock to see; yes, I know; in the newspaper!"

Madame Legrande sympathised with her old school friend about her daughter's life being invaded by the press, camped outside her apartment. Madame Legrande asked her how her daughter was coping with having had her love affair so publicly splattered across the tabloids.

"No, I do not know what kind of a man would say such false things about Avril," Madame Legrande said into her mobile. "Yes, yes, yes…only a dishonourable type. Then again, Moni, men these days, are nothing like those we once knew in our youth."

Madame Legrande listened further. Clearly, Moni Goumas needed to get things off her chest. M'sieur Pom and I sat patiently. Madame Legrande wished Madame Goumas well and hung up.

"There's no love affair. Moni Goumas said it was very presumptuous of that horrible man to say that he was in anyway involved in a duplicitous romance with her morally upright daughter. Avril has locked herself in her apartment. She's taken leave from work. When it dies down, she'll quietly take the train to Paris, to spend time with an old school friend, to get away from all the kerfuffle."

M'sieur Pom and I left, wishing Madame Legrande a pleasant afternoon.

"Keep me posted, M'sieur Pom. This could run all week."

It did.

Madame Legrande told me that Moni Goumas had rung her back a day later, concerned for her daughter trapped inside her apartment by a media throng on the footpath outside.

"Dougay, I'm going to go over to see if Avril is okay. Moni can't go, as she'll no doubt be recognised. But the media does not know me and my connection to Avril's mother. I intend taking the poor girl some groceries."

"Madame, you can't go by yourself."

"I was hoping you'd say that, Dougay."

I hailed a passing taxi outside *L'Opera Mozart*. We stopped off at a supermarket, buying milk, ham, cheese and the ubiquitous bread stick. Moni Goumas was correct. There was a throng of bored cameramen and journalists hanging about, cluttering the footpath outside her daughter's apartment. I recognised Mimi Benoit in amongst them.

"G'day, Mimi," I said in my broadest Australian accent, hoping to come across as an innocent abroad.

She looked at me, finally realising. "Oh, you're the man with the Mozart exhibition." So much for the memorable nature of my newspaper interview.

"What's going on?" I asked with impressionable wide eyes.

"Corrupt public servant has gone to ground. We need a statement. The public is crying out to know."

I walked towards Madame Legrande and the entrance.

"Are you going inside?" Mimi Benoit called out, following, dragging out her notepad from her jacket pocket.

"Yes, Madame's long-time friend is recovering in there. He only got back from hospital yesterday. We're dropping in supplies for him." Half lies are the best form of disguise.

Mimi put away the notepad. Madame Legrande pushed the intercom and spoke. The door buzzed and we entered, Madame Legrande saying to me, "You tell bigger stories than my two sons combined."

"I'll take that as a compliment, Madame."

"It wasn't meant that way. Wait here, Dougay. I don't wish to alarm Avril. Too many strangers, you know." Madame Legrande carried the groceries into the elevator.

After twenty minutes, I walked Madame Legrande back through the media pack, now completely uninterested in us.

"How is she, Madame?"

"Not good. She doesn't know what all the fuss is about. She says that man wanted to donate money for a park bench in memory of his mother. They were up there inspecting possible sites. I told Avril it would all die down in a day or two. I don't think she believed me."

***

Jules had planted his seed well because concern was manifesting itself in the community and the public was beginning to be heard. Editorials and opinionated broadcasts were focusing concern for the city's threatened green space.

M'sieur Pom read to me readers' letters to the editor. They all said basically the same thing: "Keep your hands off our park!"

Then the next day, he made a point of telling me, "It is turning nasty. Let me read you this letter to the editor. *Public servants are trusted employees of the government. They are installed to protect the interests of the general public, not collude with property developers. Avril Goumas is a disgrace to her position, to her stature in society and to all decent morally guided women.*"

"Ouch," I said. "That's savage and personal." Remembering what Madame Legrande had said about Avril not fully comprehending the situation around her, I wondered how she felt about becoming the focus of such public condemnation. "Who'd write such a thing, M'sieur Pom?"

He looked again at the letter. "Madame Felice Ardoin."

Felice Ardoin? I didn't say anything, however *Ardoin* was the name used be Felicity Deschamps the first time I met her. And *Felice* is short for…

"Keep me posted, M'sieur Pom."

He did.

Overnight, the media changed tack from concern over the protection of the park, to an outright assault on Avril Goumas. The letters, articles, and editorials focused in on her and not on Paul Villan and Felicity and Pierre Deschamps. That letter had been carefully worded and planted by someone who understood politics inside out. It was a cruel, cunning ploy on the part of Felicity Deschamps.

Avril, it's time to head to your friend's apartment in Paris, I thought to myself as I bid M'sieur Pom, "Good morning."

The next morning, M'sieur Pom told me Avril Goumas had been stood down from her position, without pay, pending an enquiry.

Letters to the editor now screamed: 'Victory for people power!'

Felicity Deschamps may have distanced herself from the photograph Jules had sent to Mimi Benoit, and from the fallout around Avril Goumas; however, her attempt at rezoning the park had been nipped in the bud. Jules had struck his match, singeing a hole in Pierre and Felicity Deschamps' first attempt at realising their economic dream.

I vowed never to owe Jules money and not pay it. *Well done, Jules, well done!* I mimed a toast to a successful outcome for the 'good guys.'

If only that was to be the case.

Chapter 16

My phone was ringing by my bed. "What time is it?" I mumbled, half asleep. I fumbled my mobile, finally getting it to my ear.

"Dougay!" Claude whispered, afraid. "Someone's broken in. I heard a window smash and…"

That's all I heard. I dropped the phone on my bed, stepped into my old slippers and threw on my goat herder's jacket over my pyjamas.

I ran. I stopped to gather my keys. I was out my apartment door, flying down the stairs, across the foyer, half-sliding into the locked front door. I found my key, opened it and fell into the dark street, accelerating past Place Mozart.

Turning the corner, I pulled up in front of *L'Opera Mozart*, using my outstretched arms against the building to stop my run. There was a torch light flashing about inside. I opened the locked front door and bolted straight for the light.

Torches do not shine by themselves, suspended magically in the air, so I lunged in the darkness at the end of the beam and tackled a man to the ground. I put the knee in. I pushed up, lifting my left fist. I slammed it into his guts. I hit him with another. I ripped at his face and tore at his balaclava.

Another man had come around the counter from the cash register and he hit me from behind with one of my new chairs! I was knocked sideways and down, like that time in the outdoor café in Aubagne. Would I ever learn?

The tackled thief struggled to his feet. I threw out a fist and only managed to collect him with a thump to his ass! He fell to one knee.

I sprung up and hit the chair-wielding thug with the hardest, most savage blow I could manage from such an unbalanced position. He grunted on impact. I lunged at him, ripping at his face. His balaclava shifted, revealing a portion of face, though it didn't come off.

He flailed at me, and at his face, trying to find the eyeholes. As the thief on the floor pulled my leg up and out, I lost balance and fell.

They fled to the café's front door. I found my feet. The two men ran out and I followed. On the footpath outside, realising I'd never catch them, I screamed, "I took a photo! I have your faces on my mobile, you assholes!"

I hadn't. I'd left my phone back in my room! Ah well, if you can't leave your mark on them physically, then leave them with a little mental concern to be going on with.

I found Claude sitting slumped on the stairs leading up to his flat.

"I'm okay," he managed to say. "Stomach hurts. I've been winded. They hit me when I confronted them."

"Come on, Claude," I said, placing my hands behind his shoulders, "let's get you inside." I lifted him to his feet. He gingerly climbed the last few steps.

I'd never been inside Claude's apartment. The plain wooden door opened into a large living room with a kitchen off to the side, its window looking over the alley. Bedrooms were down a corridor.

The large window of the living room overlooked *L'Opera Mozart's* entranceway. Claude has expensive taste, which is not evident in the café below. We sat in comfortable chairs, facing each other.

"I heard the window smash," he said. "It woke me."

"Which window?"

"The one over the exit door, leads into the alley. One of them must have slid through the top, because I heard the exit bars push open. I called you and they were immediately on the stairs. They came here first before hitting the cash register downstairs.

"I shouted at them from the top. One charged up and hit me. I fell a few steps, holding on. I didn't wish to fall the entire flight. They couldn't have cared less. They stepped over me like a piece of dog shit on the footpath. One of them put the boot in." Claude indicated his lower torso.

"As a young man, Dougay, I'd played rugby. I've been in my fair share of close physical contact, but this kick knocked the wind out of me. I couldn't get anything functioning properly, couldn't get to my feet and certainly couldn't call out.

"It didn't take them long to find what they were looking for. I never expected this—this invasion, so I've never really hidden things. They were prying open the cash register downstairs when you burst in. You know I only keep the float in there. The takings I keep up here with me."

Something dawned on him. "It's Thursday night. I always do the banking Friday. They took everything—everything we've made this past week. And what a week we had,

Dougay. Your exhibition brought in all those extra people. Do you think they knew?"

I shrugged. I had no idea. However, I began joining those old reliable dots. Dot one was that detective from Aix-en-Provence flashing his torch out back, supposedly checking on security. Dot two was Milos having had his bar broken into on a previous Thursday night.

"Glass of water?" I asked Claude. He nodded, and I went and filled two glasses.

While the water fell from the tap, I concentrated on the half-seen face of the first thief. Dot three! Aix-en-Provence. Tonight's thieves were those two cops who'd thumped me and tossed me into a woman's car, after I'd woken from a night on a garbage tip on the outskirts of their jurisdiction.

Now I knew what they were doing here in Nice. What had Pierre Legrande said to me about those three cops?

Avoid them, Dougay. If you don't, you'll be scraping shit off your shoes for weeks. Well, I hadn't avoided them and they'd certainly left their shit on Claude.

I handed the glass to him. "Don't worry about the money. In the morning, report the robbery to the police."

"They'll never find them."

"No, maybe not. However, you'll need a case number from the police to claim on the insurance. Pay for the new pane of glass."

Claude looked at me, surprised. "You're not just a pretty face, are you, Dougay?"

Claude continued to worry about losing the takings of such a strong week. I placated his worry by suggesting we could hold over the *Mozi-Art 1.0* exhibition for two or three weeks. The demand was there for it, and we'd be able to make up for what had been stolen tonight.

I stayed with him for close to an hour, until I felt he was okay and sleep would soon take him. I returned home to bed, saying nothing to Louise, wishing and hoping that somehow, I could find those three mongrel dogs and implement some of my own old-fashioned revenge.

Chapter 17

I had a fitful night's sleep, having gone over and over the break in at the café and wondering how I'd find those thieves.

Is it worth my while going back to Aix-en-Provence and confronting them? They're cops, Dougay! Be sensible. You'll only come off second best and who'd believe your story anyway? Certainly not fellow cops!

After 8am, my mobile rang. I was half-undressed when I'd heard it, my leg caught in my pyjama pants. I hopped to it. It was Francine. Some women have great timing.

"You're ringing early," I said, stepping out and righting myself.

Before I could go on, she cut in with, "I'm not missing you."

I didn't tell her I was now standing half-naked in the morning light, a slight ache still on me from last night's altercation. Francine already knew enough about me.

"It's early I know," she apologised. "I have a job for you. Can you drop by at nine?"

I was there, as requested. I took the elevator up to the third floor and turned left. The young receptionist hadn't made it into work yet.

Francine had the strangest look on her face. "You won't believe this. I don't know whether to laugh or cry."

"You'd better explain."

"Okay. A man and a woman have had a monumental bust-up. She's taken the only thing of value that belonged to him, probably out of spite. It's his family photograph album— photos from before they hooked up."

"She's taken his family album?" I asked for clarification.

"Yes. He has taken out a Domestic Violence Protection Order against her."

"Him, against her?" I questioned, surprised.

"Yes, he wants his photo album back, and that's what you've got to go and get."

"Okay."

"Sit back," she said.

"You're not going to climb…"

"This is business, Dougay." She looked at me, a slight smile of enjoyment coming to her lips. She paused, leaving me momentarily dangling on her fishing line. "My client is Henri Lemoine."

"Lemoine!" I laughed out loud. "Lemoine! And Lemoine's Tart has taken his family album?"

"Yes."

"And he's taken a Domestic Violence Protection Order out against her!"

"Yes!"

Henri Lemoine, though I never knew his first name, had been my first 'client' for Francine. He had to sign a legal document. He'd refused. I'd thumped him. He'd agreed.

The woman I'd dubbed as Lemoine's Tart, on a return visit, came at me with a carving knife, missed, and ended up stabbing her dodgy meal ticket in his leg!

I slapped my knees and rose from the chair. "I'll go get it."

"Where are you going?"

"To Lemoine's place, if I can find it, behind all that junk out front."

"No, she's not there. She's moved out." Francine reached for her business cards. "Here." She took one and wrote deliberately on the back: 'Photos!' "That's just in case you forget what you're supposed to be doing."

She laughed, cheekily. I love it when women toy with me. Then she wrote the address. I recognised it. It was the street the woman's brother lived in.

The brother and his pal had assaulted me one night, and as retribution, I stuck four toothpicks into the valves of their car's tyres. The car was an old Renault, classy. The brother and his pal weren't.

I noted the number—37. I held the card in my palm as I thanked her and left, leaving her with a cheery, "Once more, Francine, unto the fray."

Emerging onto the street outside, I was set upon and hammered to the ground by two assailants. Their blows were relentless. I felt a fist smash into my left kidney! Then as I struggled to remain upright, my rib cage exploded from behind, as something like a police truncheon smacked into it.

I couldn't do anything other than tuck in my arms and roll into a ball for protection. A savage kick whipped into my side. I managed to get myself against the wall of the building and there I lay as still as I could, pretending I was beaten. Who was I kidding? I was well and truly beaten. My pockets were searched.

"No phone!" I heard a voice shout to someone further away.

Another voice said, "What's this?" He grabbed Francine's business card from my hand.

"Hey, boss!" The first voice called out.

"Photos!" The second voice screamed, reading the card. "There's an address!"

The two ran off down the street to a third man. I squinted. It was that detective from Aix-en-Provence, Bernard St Duprey.

A passer-by leant down to help me to my feet. He wasn't rushing things, thank goodness. He was not so much holding me, as stopping me from falling. I managed to ease myself up from the waist.

"Thanks, mate, I'll be okay now."

"Are you sure, Monsieur?" My Good Samaritan asked.

I stretched my back and rubbed my throbbing kidney. I put one foot in front of the other, slowly making it to the end of the street, only noticeably zigzagging three times! I didn't think anything was broken inside me—bones, muscles, nor plumbing.

I headed to Lemoine's Tart's brother's place for the family album, thankful that those two assholes hadn't kicked me in the family jewels.

I turned into the brother's street in time to see, up ahead, Detective St Duprey relentlessly pounding on the door of number 37. I eased into the shadow of a doorway to observe further. I heard a shouting female voice, muffled as it approached him from the inside. Then I heard a clearly defined, "Fuck off! I've told you before!"

The door flung open. That wild-eyed woman, Lemoine's Tart, lunged at the detective before he had any idea what was happening. He staggered back, clutching his chest. She stood holding her ground, wildly wielding the bloodied knife and screaming invective.

Detective St Duprey was trying to stay upright, as if falling would give way to death. Randomly crying out to try to combat the excruciating pain, with one hand he was holding his chest, and with the other reaching for a handkerchief. Finding it, he held it against the wound to stem the bleeding through his shirt, though he couldn't stay standing. He fell.

The sight of all this had trapped his two accomplices, as if suspended in time. Then they snapped out of it and charged the crazy woman—brawn to the fore, their tiny brains having been left back in their hotel room. She lashed out at them, giving her best impersonation of Scaramouche, lunging and parrying, keeping them momentarily at bay.

Never try to grab a knife by the blade! They both flung their hands back, wringing them, flinging blood into the air! The more they violently wrung their lacerated hands, the more the blood flung higher and wider, and the more they cussed and screamed. It couldn't have happened to two more deserving chaps!

All the while Lemoine's Tart screamed over the top of their protests, "Fuck off! Fuck off!"

The taller of the two moonlighting cops again charged the woman, his hands attempting to grab her by the throat. In doing so, he flung blood all over her face.

"Yuk!" The crazed woman screamed, and ducking his reach, lashed out again, the knife cutting across the stomach of her attacker. He screamed and fell back clutching his guts, next to Bernard St Duprey clutching his.

A neighbour was beside me, horrified at what he'd also witnessed. "Call an ambulance," I said. "I've left my phone at home!"

As he reached for his mobile, I ran across the street. The tall cop was on his back, the life draining from him.

"Put down the knife!" I screamed at Lemoine's Tart. "Put down the knife!"

The savageness in my voice seemed to hold her there momentarily. It was just long enough for me to clench my left fist and unleash a savage blow to the back of her hand. The knife dropped and she fell back against the wall of the building, as if the weight of the deadly blade had been holding her equilibrium.

"The ambulance is on its way," said the neighbour, now beside me, one foot either side of the writhing detective.

I knelt beside the seriously wounded cop. His eyes started to turn upward. I didn't like the look of that. I began pumping his heart. I called to the neighbour, "Kick the knife away."

He began to bend towards it. "No! You don't want your fingerprints on it. Kick it away!" He did so. I kept on pumping the cop's chest. "Stand between her and the knife!" I shouted to the neighbour. "If she tries anything, hit her!"

"I can't hit a woman!"

"If you don't, you'll be down here, stabbed like the others!" The neighbour stood between the knife and the crazy woman slumped against the wall. I kept pumping. The cop's heart gave a kick, and I eased off. His eyes rolled forward to where they belonged. I left him to go to the detective.

"Hang in there," I said to Bernard St Duprey, "the ambulance is on its way."

"I'm okay," uttered the detective, clutching the bloodied handkerchief against his chest. He didn't look okay.

Lemoine's Tart screamed, followed by a breathless, "Phoar!" She'd tried to get to her feet to continue her mayhem. The neighbour had taken my advice and thumped her on the chest. "Sorry!" He apologised.

She fell back down. "Bastard!" She hurled back at him. "I'm going to sue you!"

"How's my brother?" asked Bernard St Duprey.

I checked back on the cop. "No!" I called out, for his eyes were once again rolling back. "Come on, mate, hang in there!" I didn't pump his chest too hard, as I didn't want to cause damage to his rib cage. Instead, I pumped vigorously, like I'd been taught all those years ago by the lifesavers on Bondi Beach.

"Where are you going?" I shouted back towards the street. The third thief was trying to stumble away from the scene up the footpath. "You're leaving a trail of blood. You'll be easier to track than Hansel and Gretel in the woods!" He thought about that and stopped.

In the distance, I could hear the sirens approaching.

"Come on, mate! Hang in there!" I whispered into my patient's ear. "You can do this!" I kept pumping.

The sirens were getting closer. I stopped pumping the cop's chest, for again his eyes had righted themselves. I stayed kneeling beside him in case his eyes decided to flip again.

Paramedics arrived beside me with oxygen and a stretcher. "We'll take over now."

Chapter 18

I sat off to the side of the Emergency Service's activity, hoping Raphael Legrande might be the detective sent to investigate. He was.

"What are you doing here?" He asked, not believing his good luck, or misfortune, as he walked towards me sitting just outside the string of police tape. "That doesn't look good for you," he said, indicating the blood on my hands.

"I'll tell you what I know if you tell me what you know," I teased.

"I told you before, Dougay, it doesn't work like that. How are you involved in this?"

"As an innocent bystander. She's the one who wielded the knife." I indicated Lemoine's Tart sprawled in the front doorway of her brother's home, a crazed look in her eyes.

"He's correct, Detective," the neighbour said. "I saw everything."

"That bastard hit me!" Lemoine's Tart screamed. "I want him arrested!"

A uniformed policeman lifted the handcuffed woman from the doorway. "I'm laying assault charges!" Lemoine's Tart was led away to a patrol car. "Fuck off! Leave me alone!

I have rights!" Another officer walked behind, carrying her blood stained knife in a plastic evidence bag.

"I'll need a statement," Raphael said to the neighbour.

"Of course."

The two walked off a little, Raphael taking out his pencil and note pad. After that, he took my statement.

A braided uniformed, grey haired policeman arrived, strutting with authority.

"Detective Legrande," the imposing figure said.

"Sir," replied Raphael. The two walked off and put their heads together. After a while, they returned to me and the neighbour, the high-ranking officer looking at me with disdain. "Inside the house, Detective Legrande, is that part of the crime scene?"

"No, Sir, only out here."

"Take this man inside and wash off that blood. We don't need him scaring the neighbours."

The neighbour spoke up. "His deeds should earn him a medal. He saved their lives, pumping their hearts. He's a hero!"

Raphael didn't believe so. "Do you live nearby, Sir?"

"Yes, over there."

"Go home, Sir. Clean yourself up."

The neighbour needed no second piece of advice. He set off and Raphael took me inside to the kitchen. After washing my hands thoroughly, I asked, "What time do you finish work this evening? I'll be working at *L'Opera Mozart*. There could be a cold beer in the fridge with your name on it."

Detective Legrande studied me curiously. "What exactly do you know that's not in your statement?"

"Cold beer; 6pm; *L'Opera Mozart*. I have a back-story you might be interested in hearing."

"Mmm." He considered my offer. "'Back' story? What's the 'front' story?"

"Those bastards broke into *L'Opera Mozart* last night, bashed Claude and stole the entire week's takings."

"Mmm." Raphael was doing a lot of contemplating lately. He looked at his watch. "I'll see you at six." He turned to go.

"Where are you off to? Are you finished here?"

Raphael said nothing, merely giving me an enigmatic smile.

The two ambulances were on their way to the hospital and there were only a few forensic people taking photographs of the aftermath. No one was interested in me, so I walked back to Francine's office. The receptionist was now at her desk. On seeing me open the door, her eyes brightened.

"You're okay! Trouble, I hear, downstairs."

"Something like that."

"Go right in," she said.

"Are you okay?" Francine asked, standing from behind her desk, with concern. "I heard you were assaulted on the street below."

"It was nothing." I waved away her concern, as I sat opposite her. *Nothing compared to what ensued*, I thought.

"I went down, but you'd gone."

"How do you know what happened?"

"The gentleman who helped you to your feet, is a client. He was coming here for his appointment."

I sat back, stretching my sore legs, rubbing my aching arms. I think I could still feel some of the adrenalin coursing through my blood stream. Something was responsible for the way I was thinking.

Francine sat back down, keeping her eyes on me and my false devil-may-care nonchalance.

"So," she said, "no family album? It's the only time you've returned empty handed."

"Sorry, the woman went crazy and stabbed a couple of out-of-town cops. I'll have to go back another time. Or else you could tell Lemoine to go around there and fetch the photo album himself, as I'm sure she won't be there. Her residential address has been moved to the police station."

"I can still pay you," she said, reaching for her purse. "I never want to see you go without."

"It's okay. I won't starve this week. *Mozi-Art 1.0* is a national sensation!"

"Yes, congratulations are in order. I feared it may have back-fired on you, though you've proved me wrong."

I looked at her. I closed her office door. The adrenalin had not subsided. "Francine, please stand." She looked at me puzzled, though she did so. I walked around the desk and kissed her.

"In this office, business is business, Dougay," she said in her familiar warning tone.

"Not today, it isn't."

"Aren't you injured?" She asked. I ignored her question.

I kissed her a second time, passionately. She didn't resist. Then after separating from our mutual embrace, she gently pushed me away and went into the outer office. There she told the receptionist to take an early lunch. She handed the girl twenty euro. The kid was out the door like a rocket leaving Cape Canaveral.

Francine returned to me. She swept stationery to the floor. It clanged like bells announcing a joyous event.

"Take out your hair, Francine. Slowly, very slowly and gently shake it from side to side."

Francine smiled and complied. "I hope it's going to be longer than twelve minutes!" She dragged me onto the desk, the sight of countless legal transactions. I couldn't say if our transaction was legal or not, though I did hear Francine utter something about it being the first of its kind transacted there.

"Where are you going?" She asked, once we'd replaced our dishevelled clothing.

"I've a broken window to board up and then I'm going to buy a laptop!"

***

"What's that?" M'sieur Pom asked, as I carried in my brand new piece of equipment. It was the first thing I'd bought through a regular, legal outlet, and not through Remy, with his dodgy connections. I was looking forward to turning it on.

"It's a laptop! It's time I became a modern man living at the cutting edge of technology."

"Are you going to set it up yourself? Or do you know a ten-year-old child?" M'sieur Pom asked, laughing at his gag.

"Is it complex?"

"Have you ever owned one?"

"No."

"Come on," he said. We rode the elevator up to my apartment. After a long time, a very long time, he showed me how the emails worked.

"Are you going to buy a printer?" He asked on his way out.

"A printer? How much do they cost?"

"Dougay, welcome to the financial black hole of technology." He left.

I found the email address for Sue-Lin Cambridge, which was the only one I had written down, and tried not to omit a 'dot', as I sent her an email saying 'Hi!' and informing her I was now online, like the rest of mankind, who had access to a functioning electricity grid.

***

Detective Raphael Legrande walked into *L'Opera Mozart,* a little after 6pm. Dr Armand was not with him. Perhaps she was saving some poor soul, who'd been wheeled into the hospital's Emergency Department. I had an ironic thought, wondering if she'd sewn up the wounds of those three from Aix-en-Provence.

"Why are people queuing?" Raphael asked, looking at the line emerging from the archway leading into the back room.

"They wish to spend time viewing the exhibition."

"What? Those crude and violent paintings you revealed a couple of Sunday nights ago?"

"The very same; people are lining up to see them."

"People are lining up to see them?"

"Is there an echo out here?" I quipped, putting down two cold beers on an outside table. "At last, *L'Opera Mozart* has lifted its head above the crowd."

A woman stopped by us on her way out, saying, "Lovely photograph in the newspaper a few weeks back."

I smiled, "*Merci.*"

"It's a wonderful idea, congratulations," she further enthused. "I find most art is too pretentious for words."

Her male partner added, "Yes! It's too firmly stuck up its own ass!" I think he'd found the words she was looking for. They bid me *au revoir* and drifted off.

I returned my focus to Raphael. "A shame a detective and two off-duty policemen were stabbed today," I said, with mock concern. "Will Detective St Duprey survive?"

"Yes. A night or two in hospital, then he'll be out. I have that on good advice." Dr Armand had attended to them after all.

"I realise that the crazy woman can't go around knifing people knocking on her door, and particularly out of uniform policemen, but Bernard St Duprey will have a lot of explaining to do."

Raphael sipped his beer. "We wait with anticipation his concocted tale. So, Dougay, what's the full back-story?"

"Okay, join the dots."

"Why not play snakes and ladders, as well?"

I ignored him. "Dot one: a man steals ten euro from this very table. Dot two: I saw you sharing a coffee over in Le Piol with that man. Dot three: you told me his name was Detective Bernard St Duprey. Dot four: I found that detective in the rear lane shining his torch up at the building. He claimed he was checking it out for 'security reasons'.

"Dot five: *Vlatava-Elbe* was broken into and robbed. The thieves got access through the rear window. Dot six: As I said, we were robbed last night—same MO. I fought off two of the thieves. They got away with our entire week's takings. Foolishly, I told them I'd taken their photo when I hadn't, because I didn't want them to think they'd got away scot free. They'd believed me.

"Dot seven: The lawyer, Francine Delange, hires me to get some photos back for a client. I'm assaulted upon leaving her office by these off-duty cops and they ignorantly take the card bearing the hand written address and head off there. They thought that was where the incriminating photos were. Why are you cops such dumb asses?"

"Stick to the dot points," warned Raphael.

"Dot eight: They knock on number 37. It is opened by a woman with a knife fixation, who greets Detective Bernard St Duprey with a stab to the chest. The other two dolts charge her and get lacerated fingers and stomach for their trouble. All in all, it's a reasonable result for us good guys."

"Is that what we are?" Raphael asked, slyly. "Good guys?"

"Well, I am!" I smiled cheekily. He groaned.

"Raphael, there's no proof about their thieving activities, and I officially didn't see their faces, though maybe your superiors need to grill those three as to why they were so far from home."

Raphael drained his beer.

"Ironies of ironies," I said. "Remember the time I was bashed and left on that garbage dump outside Aix-en-Provence?"

Raphael nodded, wondering where I was now heading with the conversation.

"I never told you this, but when I came to, there was a sachet of cocaine up my ass. I got rid of that very quickly. However, when I was stumbling off down the road, I was stopped by those two cops and immediately searched—up my ass! They'd been tipped off.

"Then this morning, after they assaulted me, I saw them receive fate's retribution. Kismet is a wonderful thing. Now you're up to date."

"After he did all that to you, you still pumped his heart, saving his life. Most people would have walked away."

"A long time ago, I realised that I'm not like most people."

"Your kind heartedness, one day, will get you into trouble."

"I think it already has."

Raphael stood. "Come show me that broken window where they got in."

"I can't prove it was them. It'll be my word against them."

"Show me the window, Dougay."

I took Raphael out back through the people milling around the paintings. He looked up at the piece of ply board above the exit door. "When's the glass man coming?"

"Tomorrow."

"It's busy in here," he said, indicating the cafe's back room. He leant against the exit bar and opened the door. "Step outside for a moment."

"Why? You're not planning on kicking the shit out of me in the back alley, are you?"

"What? And have you tell my mother? Come on."

We walked into the alley and I left the exit door ajar so we'd be able to get back inside.

Raphael looked around. As always, the alley was deserted. He put his hand against his chest.

"Are you going to shoot me?"

"Shut up, Dougay, and listen." Raphael stepped into me, his mouth to my ear. "You're not the only one who can join dots. I made some subtle unofficial enquiries and found the small hotel where Bernard St Duprey was staying."

He reached inside his jacket and passed me a thick envelope. "I wasn't there. I didn't search his room. And I didn't find this in his luggage."

I took a peek inside. "Dear God!" I whispered. "Did you take a ten percent commission? A finder's fee?"

"I'm not a corrupt cop, Dougay. I get my kick out of righting wrongs."

I laughed. "Claude will be ecstatic."

"Let's go back inside," said Raphael, taking me by the arm. "I didn't realise I could get so thirsty solving crime."

Chapter 19

The first email I received was from Sue-Lin Cambridge. She was back in Melbourne for a month, before heading off to the Caribbean for a photo shoot. Delighted I was now online, she brought me up to date with the Australian footy results and thanked me once again for walking her home the night of the art event. For all her fame and fortune, could she be lonely and in need of a confidant? I couldn't say. I only knew, whatever emails she'd send, I'd answer.

Getting excited about electronic possibilities, I called Mary-Anne and left her a voice message, carefully quoting her my email address. I sent Francine my address and she replied with an automatically generated: *I'm out of the office at the moment.*

My initial enthusiasm for email was being dampened. M'sieur Pom said I'd get used to that.

I could feel summer wanting to knock on the door, so one morning before breakfast I opened it, and headed to the beach. Holding my breath against the chill, I fell in and swam as fast as I could to relieve the shock. I'd taken the plunge and was swimming once again. Though for now, it may not be every morning.

About ten metres off shore, swimming towards the airport, I came to the end of my usual 'lap'. I eased up and treaded water. Before I turned around, I saw further on from me flashing lights on shore.

I swam directly out to sea another twenty or so metres, enabling me to see down the beach from a better angle. An ambulance and police cars were as close to the water's edge as they could manage.

I turned back and completed two laps, returning. I looked down the beach again. A body was being lifted from the water. *People need to learn to swim,* I thought. I turned and swam away, completing my morning's half hour.

***

I accompanied Madame Legrande to the funeral of Avril Goumas.

From where the taxi dropped us, we walked a little, Madame Legrande threading her arm through mine. "I cannot begin to feel what it must be like to lose a child," she confided. "Most parents believe they'll die before their children do. I certainly hope I do."

The chapel came into sight, Madame Legrande holding me back. "I remember Moni saying that as a child, Avril was delicate."

"Delicate, Madame? In what way?"

"She was greatly affected by events around her. Even things she had no control over, she would deeply personalise. Little wonder the pressure on her these past few days had affected her so."

Madame Legrande didn't have to say anything further.

The funeral was in a small chapel attached to the undertaker's premises. The church Avril had been baptised in had refused her mother their services as suicide was against the Lord's laws, and therefore, Avril could not be blessed and prepared for entry into heaven.

There was no media throng outside. They were moving onto the next story, off someplace else harassing some other target, having wiped their hands of any responsibility for the public pressure they'd put the young woman through. There'd be no public apology coming forth from a media baron over the demise of Avril Goumas.

Yes, I confess, we'd all jumped the gun. I shouldn't have asked Jules to get his camera out and take a photograph of her up at *Park de L'Eco-Vallee.* I should have minded my own business. Since the photograph had been published, no evidence had come to light of Avril having taken an underhanded euro.

An official funeral car drew up and the undertaker's assistant opened the rear door, helping Moni Goumas out. Upon seeing Madame Legrande, she crossed to her, holding herself upright, maintaining dignity. The two old friends fell into each other, hugging.

To her credit, Mimi Benoit came, and didn't try to interview Madame Goumas or Madame Legrande. She nodded sombrely to me and I returned the gesture. She made a subtle note on her small pad.

I guess whatever she'd be writing would turn up in the morning's paper, buried somewhere, well away from the previous front page's screaming headlines and repeated photograph.

Among the handful in attendance, I only recognised Madame Petain and Avril's two other luncheon companions. They were visibly shaken, true friends to the end.

In the front pew, Moni Goumas sat between Madame Legrande and me, the casket raised on its stand at eye level two metres in front of us. Sitting so near, I couldn't get my mind off Avril—dead, just there in front of me, lying stretched out. Recorded organ music began to sound quietly in the chapel.

Waiting for the celebrant to take her position beside the coffin, I heard a footfall behind. I turned to see Paul Villan slide into a back pew. I was pleased he'd come to pay his last respects and possibly ask forgiveness for his small, yet pivotal role in the death of the young woman.

Felicity Deschamps did not appear.

The celebrant stood behind a lectern off to the side and began to speak into the microphone as the organ music faded away, timed perfectly.

I relived what little I knew of Avril and of Jules and me following her to the park and again his taking of those photographs. I didn't blame Jules. He could not have predicted the impact his releasing that photograph to Mimi Benoit would have. And I believed Mimi had no inkling of the consequences of its publication.

She'd been wishing to expose possible corruption, not set in motion a tragedy. I'm sure they both believed they were saving a park, though Jules also would have thought of the added bonus of wanting to disrupt the connivances of Felicity Deschamps.

Consequences, I thought. *What a tragic mess of interconnecting desires.*

The celebrant stopped speaking and Madame Goumas stood to cross to the lectern. As she stepped across me, she stumbled, overwrought. I grabbed her and eased her back into her seat.

Once Madame Goumas calmed, Madame Legrande took the note from her hand and stood behind the lectern, reading from it in a clear, quietly passionate voice. When she'd finished, she informed the celebrant to continue with the service.

As the organ music swelled once more, Moni Goumas managed to gather enough strength to stand. I stood with her holding her upright. Guided by her, we crossed to the casket. There, with my arms around her, she held her hand out towards her daughter. Trembling, her hand touched the coffin and she broke down once more. I held her in that position until she managed to nod that she wished to be returned to the pew.

Four men in black, slowly walked from behind us, and lifted the coffin forward onto an almost hidden conveyor belt. A panel in the wall slid open, revealing flames. The coffin moved forward and in. The panel in the wall closed.

Madame Petain was standing by me, holding out her hand to Madame Goumas; to offer her condolences. With Madame Petain were Avril's other two work friends. I decided to give them a little privacy and stood. I noted Paul Villan had left the chapel.

I heard Moni Goumas sob, "I can't believe I'm never going to see Avril again."

Chapter 20

The two-week extension of the *Mozi-Art* exhibition was proving to be a success. One day, two Japanese gentlemen spent a long time in front of the paintings. Other people had to move around them, for it was the central one they'd obviously come to see. That's where they firmly stood, in front of Gabrielle's fantasy.

The younger of the two asked me in French, "Is Monsieur Dougay Roberre present this evening, please, Sir?"

I said that 'Monsieur Dougay Roberre' was me. The man translated to the elder and they both bowed. I bowed in response.

"Monsieur, I am Mister Sakaki and this gentleman is my father."

"*Bonjour*, Messieurs Sakaki." I bowed again.

"My father is a collector of pornographic prints, etchings and line drawings. This will be the first pornographic oil he will own."

"'Will' own?"

"Pardon. French verb endings are tricky. 'Would like to' own? Is that how you say it?"

"Yes, I hadn't considered selling it, Mister Sakaki."

The older man whispered in his son's ear. The son turned to me and said, "Twenty-five thousand euro. My father is not like any of the other Asian traders or businessmen you will come across; he detests bargaining. His private collection is the most extensive in the world. Twenty-five thousand euro is his only offer. If yes, we will pick it up on the day after the final evening of the exhibition. If your answer is a 'no', then we shake hands and bid you a fond farewell."

I thought for a moment. *Twenty-five thousand euro— that's ten times what I paid for it!* Without trying to sound overtly excited, I said, "Yes, you have a sale, gentlemen. I'll see you Sunday week."

We exchanged contact details. I carefully checked the email address I'd jotted down for them, still not totally familiar with the location of the dots. As they were leaving, I remembered something about the Japanese—they make wonderful beer.

"Gentlemen," I called after them, "are you in Nice for long?"

"We leave tomorrow for London, though we will return Sunday week as promised. My father is a man of his word."

"No, I don't doubt that. I trust you implicitly. Before you leave tomorrow, would you like to drink some Czech beer with me, accompanied by slivovitz?"

The younger man asked, "Tonight?"

"Now, if you like," I replied.

The younger man consulted his father.

"My father says, 'Lead the way'."

***

I hailed a taxi and we climbed in. My days of needing to always walk the streets or regularly use my multi-day travel pass were over. I asked the son if his father would like to meet the artist who painted it. He said his father would be honoured.

In the taxi, I made a phone call. "Gabi, Dougay here. An international businessman has just bought your *Mozi-Art* painting. If you'd like to meet him and thank him in person, you'll find us at *Vlatava-Elbe Bar* over in the Quartier du Port. Drinks are on me."

I then called ahead to let Milos know we were on our way and to put the slivovitz on ice, because it had to challenge my guests' love for saki.

Then I called Milovic. "Bring the wife, the sister-in-law, the brother-in-law; I'm paying."

"Where'd you come across so much money?" He asked, not believing a word I'd said.

"My dead Italian aunt named me in her will." I've got to stop lying to my friends!

With the two Japanese gentlemen happily drinking slivovitz and dark Czech beer outside with my Czech mates, I excused myself and found Milos behind his bar.

"Milos, take this," I said, handing over an envelope. "It's some of the money those thieves stole from you."

"How did you get this, Dougay?"

"No questions, Milos. Ever!"

What a night! I knew Japanese men could drink beer! I now knew they could drink slivovitz as well. Gabrielle behaved herself, which was a monumental feat considering the flowing alcohol and liberation of tongues that was going on around the table. Maybe she felt she was in the presence of some invisible *International Artistic Spotlight* and she represented *The Collective of Renowned French Artists.*

Gabi said, "Monsieur Sakaki, tell your father I am honoured that my painting will be getting pride of place, back in Japan, in his world-renowned private collection." The son translated for the father.

Towards the end of the night, the old Gabi Surmount, the one I'd come to know, reared her head. She asked the son to ask the father if he'd like to fuck the artist. The father said he would and they went off in a taxi together. I shouted after her, "Gabi! I need him alive for Sunday week, so he can pay me the money!"

***

True to their word, on the Sunday evening following the closure of *Mozi-Art 1.0*, the Sakaki men entered the cafe. I escorted them to the back room, where their painting was half wrapped, waiting for them. Upon identifying it, the old man nodded his head to his son. I completed its wrapping.

The son passed me an envelope. "Please," he said, "you must count it."

"It's not rude to count the money in front of you?" I asked, fearing I'd be damaging protocol.

"No, my father does not possess any Asian sensibilities when it comes to business."

I counted it—twenty-five thousand euro! I put it deep into my pocket. I checked that my wrapping was secure around the painting and thanked them, the three us bowing and shuffling to the door.

Later, I presented Claude with Noel Fucheon's painting.

"You paid for this, Dougay!" He protested.

"Claude, please accept it as a gift, for having believed in my crazy ideas."

"I didn't," he admitted.

"Accept it anyway."

"So," said Louise. "Are we doing this again next year? Will we hold *Mozi-Art 2.0*?"

"Yes!" We all said, and toasted each other, the artists who'd contributed, and the paintings.

I carried home Lautrelle's painting. If Gabi's painting brought twenty-five thousand without even trying to auction it, I knew Lautrelle's *Queen of the Knife*, one day would be worth a great deal more, for his painting had touched a powerful nerve in the Gallic heart.

Planning on hanging it above my bed, I propped it against the wall opposite. I flopped next to Louise on the sofa in the living room.

"Tired?" She asked. "Glad it's all over?"

"Yes."

"Will we really do it again next year?"

"We?" And before she could comment, I added, "Yes, we will."

I reached inside my jacket and withdrew the envelope from the sale of Gabi's painting. I stood and crossed to the window, fingering through the money, so Louise couldn't see. I turned back to her.

"I'd like you to have this, Louise. It's your commission from the sale of *Rondo a la Jerka*."

I handed her a bundle of notes.

She squealed, "Two and half thousand euro!"

Chapter 21

I didn't swim the next morning. I couldn't bring myself to leave the apartment before going to the bank. I tossed up whether to deposit the Sakaki cash into my account, which now possessed the embarrassingly large amount courtesy of the sale of the diamonds to Lefbvre and Massenet, or slip the twenty two and a half thousand into my safety deposit box, where the taxman could never find it. I'll let you be the judge of what I did.

I decided not to call Remy to accompany me. I took a deep breath and walked to the bank, my eyes darting every which way. I was so uncomfortable with this, I vowed that next time, if there ever was to be a next time, I'd call Remy again for protection.

Protection, that is, not so much from being thumped by a stranger from the outside, rather from my heart thumping from the inside.

When I returned to my apartment block, M'sieur Pom was at his desk. "Dougay!" He called. "Look at this! Look at this!"

He held up the front page of the morning newspaper. The headline screamed: 'Reconciliation!'

"They're back together again!"

"Who is? You'd better read it to me, M'sieur Pom."

It was announced on Saturday evening, that ex-deputy mayor, Pierre Deschamps, and his wife, Felicity, have reconciled. They have buried their differences and once again discovered the joys of what originally brought them together.

He looked up at me saying cynically, "Ain't true love grand?" We both sniggered.

Monsieur Pom read on. *Pierre Deschamps has moved back into the family home. "I was a fool," he said outside his home on Sunday morning, when reporters cornered him. "My heart belongs to Felicity. It has always belonged to Felicity. She has forgiven me, and welcomed me back into her life."*

"What are they really up to?" M'sieur Pom wondered aloud.

"Time will tell, M'sieur Pom, time will tell."

The story was continued on page six. There was another photograph. This time the loving couple was smiling happily for the camera, down on their knees, arms around each other; and around their slobbering mongrel of a dog!

***

The remainder of the day saw me measuring up my kitchen and sketching a few design ideas—placement of cupboards; nothing too elaborate, as I was still of the belief that a major relocation of pipes and electrics was not worth the money or the hassle.

In the morning, before she'd gone off to the café, Louise had been eager to help and give me her advice about the entire prospective renovation. To placate her, I'd let her hold the other end of the tape measure.

The next day, Remy drove me to a warehouse; a legitimate warehouse, which contained a higher class of goods and furniture to those he possessed.

His cousin's friend of a friend, who at one time had swapped cats with his dead brother, showed me several catalogues. I was searching for an induction cook top to be placed over a quality oven, a smallish double-sided sink and an upside-down refrigerator.

I had all the dimensions, and we mixed and matched them with the various styles in the catalogues. The cousin etc., promised to deliver them to Remy's warehouse for storage until I was ready to install them. I paid him, and Remy and I headed off to a cabinetmaker whom Remy knew.

There, the craftsman studied my sketches and measurements, showing me a set of cupboards, which he'd already made for a client, who went broke. He said I could have them at a reduced rate. Checking the measurements, he added that he'd only need to cut down two of the four floor cabinets to fit my sketched puzzle. The two overhead cabinets could be successfully screwed to the wall, above and to the side of the sink's placement, without alteration.

All done, Remy and I started to leave.

"What colour splash backs and bench tops were you thinking about?" The cabinetmaker asked.

***

Back in the truck, Remy said, "With that new induction cook top, you're going to need new frying pans and saucepans."

"Really?" I asked.

"The old ones aren't compatible with the new technology."

"Do you have a cousin or an aunt…?"

He spun the truck 180 degrees.

As we walked in, the saleslady, inside the kitchenware shop, exclaimed, "Hello, Uncle Remy!"

Remy kissed her, and they chatted about her husband and their two children, now happily away in Paris at university. I coughed.

"Oh yes," said Remy, "we're looking for pots and pans to go with a new induction cook top."

She walked us away from the door and further into the store. "This is what you're after," she said, giving me one to hold. It was heavier than the old ones.

Suddenly, a man snatched something from the counter and ran. The sales lady screamed, "Stop! Thief!"

I spun around and let fly with the frying pan. It hit the thief between his shoulder blades. He fell to the floor, collapsing over the old security guard, still half-asleep in his chair by the door.

"You should make those frying pans in the shape of a boomerang," I informed the sales lady.

"Why's that?" she asked.

"Well, your uncle Remy is going to have to walk over there and pick it up."

***

Mary-Anne rang. She must have been in a meeting, because the conversation did not last, other than to give me her proposed date of arrival back on the Cote d'Azur. I wrote it on my notice board, next to: 'Buy Milk!' I smiled and took down the photograph of Sue-Lin, placing it in the drawer of my bedside cabinet. I remembered that I had to return that magazine to M'sieur Pom!

I knew I'd be fantasising about Mary-Anne tonight, hoping we'd once again spend a night like that night she sat near naked in front of me aboard *The Blue Dahlia*, when I thought I was going to be taken into the centre of the Mediterranean and tossed overboard.

After the conversation with Mary-Anne, I hit the link she'd sent and listened to her, using Sinatra's voice, getting a kick out of me.

She'd offered me a job! I couldn't believe it. I was going to be a second unit director, whatever that is. I agreed to supervise a cameraman and a sound recordist while they filmed the green mountains in French speaking Switzerland, for insert footage to be used in Kempenski's upcoming two movies of 'Heidi: a Young Swiss Miss'.

I said I'd even learn to yodel if it meant being paid to hang out in Switzerland and sleep with her every night. She said that she may not be required to be there. I told her to have a serious word with Kempenski. She laughed and said, "Every night with you? How come I got the booby prize?"

I love witty intelligent women!

Some nights I'd think of Avril being taken from the Mediterranean, surrounded by those flashing lights, or heading off to lunch with her friends, or walking between those trees up at *Parc de L'Eco-Vallee*. Last night, I dreamt she walked behind a palm tree and didn't emerge from the other side.

Out of the blue, I received a phone call from Sue-Lin Cambridge saying how it was wonderful to have strolled home that night; how wonderful it was to talk to someone who wasn't involved in the bullshit of her world; how wonderful it was that I was down-to-earth and even though we'd only just met—and only the once—how she'd felt that I was a true friend. I didn't tell her she'd already said all that stuff in an email. Sometimes, I love hearing repetitive versions of the truth!

Sue-Lin went on to say that she was sitting around some hotel pool being waited on, sipping from a glass of coloured umbrellas. She added that she may have had a glass or two, too many.

Yes, I silently agreed. *You sound as if you have.*

Sue-Lin said that she'd been taking basic French lessons. That she was trying to read a book about Louis and his cat. I thought that maybe one day, I could borrow it.

She left me with a sweetly disturbing thought. Her voice slowed, and she whispered carefully, in halting French, the one phrase I'd taught her: "*Une autre fois, mate!*"

Milton Keynes UK
Ingram Content Group UK Ltd.
UKHW022233081223
434043UK00012B/541